The Alchemy
of Animation

D1265367

The Alchemy of Animation

Making an Animated Film in the Modern Age

By Don Hahn

A Welcome Book

EDITIONS

NEW YORK

An Imprint of Disney Book Group

Dedicated with love to Eric Larson, who mentored a generation of Disney animators, and to all the artists past and present whose amazing work graces the pages of this book.

Copyright © 2008 Disney Enterprises, Inc. All Rights Reserved. Published by Disney Editions, an imprint of Disney Book Group. No part of this book may be reproduced or transmitted in any form or by any means, electronic or mechanical, including photocopying, recording, or by any information storage and retrieval system, without written permission from the publisher.

A Bug's Life; Cars; Finding Nemo; Lifted; Monsters, Inc.; Ratatouille; The Incredibles; Toy Story; and *Wall-E* © Disney Enterprises, Inc./Pixar Animation Studios

Roger Rabbit characters © Walt Disney Pictures /Amblin Entertainment, Inc.

TARZAN ® is a registered trademark of Edgar Rice Burroughs, Inc. All rights reserved.

Tim Burton's The Nightmare Before Christmas and *James and the Giant Peach* © Touchstone Pictures

TRON © Touchstone Pictures

Academy Award® is the registered trademark of the Academy of Motion Picture Arts and Sciences.

The American Theatre Wing owns the following registered trademarks: the Tony Award®, Tony®, the Tony Award® logo, and the Tony Award® medallion. © Copyright Tony Award Productions, 2001. All Rights Reserved.

Dolby and the double-D symbol are registered trademarks of Dolby Laboratories.

Moviola is a registered trademark of Magnasync/Moviola Corporation in the United States and other countries.

Photographs courtesy of Mike Belzer: pages 104 (middle, bottom left, bottom right); 105; 107 (top left); 109; 110; 111; 112; 113; 114; and 115

For information address Disney Editions, 114 Fifth Avenue, New York, New York 10011-5690.
Editorial Director: Wendy Lefkon
Senior Editor: Jody Revenson
Assistant Editor: Jessica Ward

Produced by Welcome Enterprises, Inc.
6 West 18th Street, New York, New York, 10011
www.welcomebooks.com
Project Director: H. Clark Wakabayashi
Design: Jon Glick, mouse + tiger

Library of Congress Cataloging-in-Publication Data on file.
ISBN 978-1-4231-0476-6

Printed in Singapore
FIRST EDITION
10 9 8 7 6 5 4 3 2 1

PAGE 1: A final clean-up of a Les Clark drawing from the "Sorcerer's Apprentice" sequence of *Fantasia*; PAGES 2–3: Color story sketch from "Sorcerer's Apprentice;" THIS PAGE: Caricature of Eric Larson by John Musker; OPPOSITE: *Fantasia* model sheet.

Table of Contents

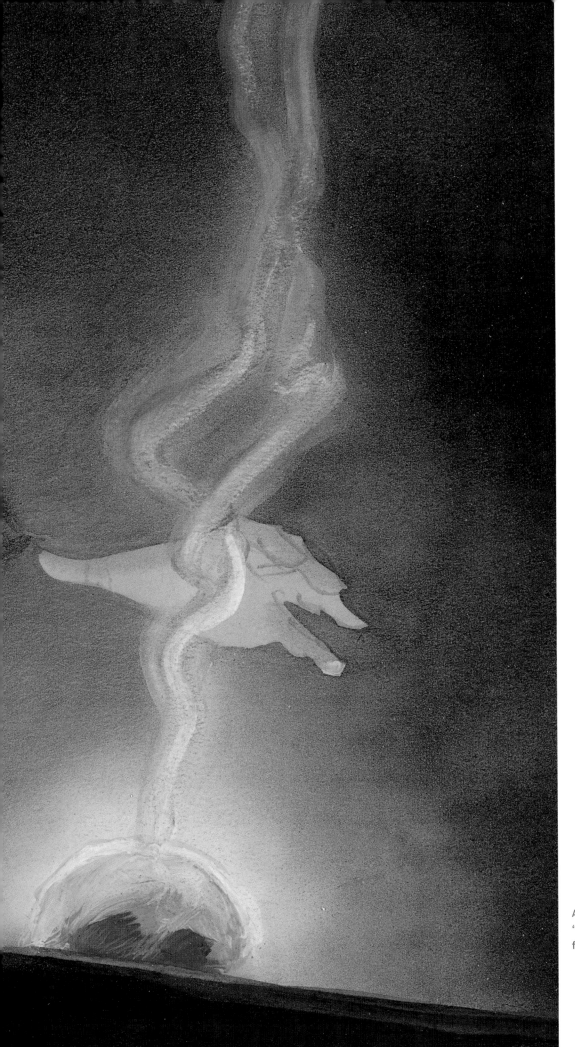

A small color study from
"The Sorcerer's Apprentice"
from *Fantasia* (1940).

Overture

Life is motion. They go together. It's no surprise that early human beings almost always tried to capture a sense of motion in their art. Motion picture animation is the modern expression of this quest for life in art. Modern animation began in the 1800s when magicians created little parlor tricks to entertain their audiences: devices with odd-sounding names such as the zoetrope or praxinoscope displayed a series of drawings on a small spinning cylindrical drum, creating the illusion of movement. Inventors, including the Lumiere brothers in France and Thomas Edison in the United States, later found that showing a series of single images, photographed on motion-picture film and projected at fast speeds, caused the brain to perceive a series of still images as moving. The physiological phenomenon behind this effect was called "persistence of vision," and it is still the underlying principle that makes films appear to be moving. This was the genesis of modern film animation.

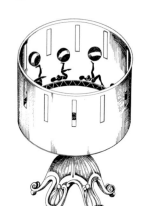

"Persistence of vision" is also a great way to describe the process of making a movie, frame by frame, over the many years of work required to make an animated feature. This phenomenon of prolonged, focused artistic collaboration is an astounding part of the animation process.

ABOVE: The zoetrope and phenakistoscope were early animation devices popular in the 19th century. They both produce an illusion of motion through a rapid series of static pictures; OPPOSITE: Eadweard Muybridge was a Victorian-era photographer who used multiple cameras to capture and analyze humans and animals in motion.

HIS FIRST FULL LENGTH FEATURE PRODUCTION

Walt Disney's

Snow White
and the Seven Dwarfs

in the Marvelous
MULTIPLANE TECHNICOLOR

©WDP

Distributed by RKO Radio Pictures, Inc.

COPYRIGHT 1937, RKO RADIO PICTURES, INC.
PROPERTY OF RKO RADIO PICTURES, INC. LEASED
FOR RESTRICTED USE ONLY... MUST BE RETURNED
TO RKO RADIO PICTURES, INC. AND MUST NOT BE
SOLD, LEASED OR GIVEN AWAY BY ANY OTHER PARTY

1-8   PRINTED IN U.S.A.

Animation has come a long way since the simple magic tricks of over a century ago. Even twenty-five years ago, animated features were less commonplace. Now, in the digital era, they are a staple of the yearly box-office blockbuster race, with dozens of animated films produced each year and entire festivals and television channels

devoted to animation. The Academy Awards now recognizes both short and feature-length animated films with an Oscar.

Animation has also spread its wings into live-action film. *Song of the South, Mary Poppins*, and *Who Framed Roger Rabbit* pioneered the combination of animation and live action, but now the lines are blurring further between animation, visual effects, and live action. The Pirates of the Caribbean and The Chronicles of Narnia series are packed with computer-generated imagery (CGI) in virtually every scene. Digital filmmaking has revolutionized our theatergoing experience, and animation is at its center. It has never been a more vibrant, living art form.

The world of animation includes many styles and techniques. Hand-drawn animation (sometimes called traditional or 2-D animation) was the vanguard of feature film production when *Snow White and the Seven Dwarfs* premiered in 1937. Digital animation started to appear in features as early as *Tron* in 1982, and the first all-computer-generated feature was *Toy Story* in 1995. Stop-motion animation, such as that used in *Tim Burton's The Nightmare Before Christmas*, is another visually spectacular technique for an animated film.

Regardless of technique, nowhere is there more magic, wonder, and illusion than in a fully animated feature film. From start to finish, the creation of an animated film is an amazing process. So if you're an aspiring artist or a fan of animation as art—or even if you've only wondered, "how'd they do that?"—then this book is for you. It's your backstage pass to see how filmmakers start with nothing but a dream, and create the wonderful reality of an animated feature.

ABOVE: Walt Disney with an early animation device called a praxinoscope; ABOVE RIGHT: *Tron* (1982) was the first movie to feature extensive sequences of computer animation; OPPOSITE: The original movie poster for *Snow White and the Seven Dwarfs* (1937) promised a Disney innovation—"marvelous multiplane Technicolor."

ACT ONE

The Idea

HATCHING AND GROWING an idea is the genesis of all films and it's probably the most important stage of the moviemaking process. Growing an idea for a movie is like farming—plant the seeds and watch them sprout. Early ideas need careful nurturing and pruning, as well as a fair amount of "persistence of vision" so they can grow into giant redwoods, otherwise the concept will wither and fade, never seeing the light of a projector bulb. Some stories—*Beauty and the Beast*, *Snow White and the Seven Dwarfs*—come from age-old fairy tales. Another film might be adapted from a book, as were *Tarzan*, *Bambi*, and *One Hundred and One Dalmatians*. For other films—*Finding Nemo*, *The Lion King*, *Ratatouille*—the story grows out of a completely original idea.

A small group of writers and visual artists led by a director and a producer, form the early-development team on a film. This team investigates the potential in a story in much the same way a journalist investigates a newspaper story. They explore the *who, what, when, where, why,* and *how* of an idea by writing, drawing, discussing, and debating. They also explore the *wow* of the story: that extra factor that makes a movie entertaining and just perfect for animation.

PRECEDING PAGES: Young Lewis's lab in a final frame from *Meet the Robinsons*; ABOVE RIGHT: Early visual development sketch of Remy from *Ratatouille*; BELOW: A simple early sketch full of emotion from *The Lion King*; OPPOSITE: A visual exploration from *Peter Pan*.

A good concept is usually rooted in a very simple core idea: lions in Africa, pirates in the Caribbean, cars, bugs, and monsters are all concepts that come with built-in audience recognition. These concepts already occupy real estate in the audience's mind. The audience comes to the theater with a certain idea about the concept and its world, and then, of course, the filmmakers have to blow the audience away with story and entertainment that exceed their expectations.

Then there are the exceptions, which carry almost no audience expectations going in. *Ratatouille* is a pretty curious title. About the only thing the audience knew when they came to the theater was the unholy combination of rats and cooking. By combining these elements in a very unexpected way, director Brad Bird exceeded audience expectations and produced one of the best-reviewed animated films ever. As director John Lasseter says, films should always "over deliver" to the audience.

CLOCKWISE FROM ABOVE: Early color explorations from *Ratatouille* and *The Lion King*; a discarded dream sequence from *The Rescuers Down Under*, and visual development art from *One Hundred and One Dalmatians*, *Meet the Robinsons*, and *Snow White and the Seven Dwarfs*; OPPOSITE: Mary Blair's color suggestion for the ballroom dance in *Cinderella*.

After establishing a strong basic concept that will take root in the audience's collective consciousness, the development team digs for strong characters with unique personalities. The story is about these characters and the emotional journey they take. We as an audience have to relate to the characters, and we should see a little bit of ourselves in a character's hopes, dreams, insecurities, and desires.

Good stories often have an underlying theme, such as the "don't judge a book by its cover" premise of *Beauty and the Beast*. All the characters—Belle, Beast, Gaston, and the enchanted objects—are one thing on the outside and something completely different on the inside. The Beast is an ugly monster with a heart of gold; Gaston is handsome, but with the heart of a monster. Other themes are very simple and direct; as in *Ratatouille*: anyone can cook.

Along with a theme, good stories also have at their core a very simple basic action. For example, you could describe the central action of *The Lion King* as "go home." Here are some more examples:

Snow White and the Seven Dwarfs:
STOP THE SPELL.

Cinderella: **GET THE PRINCE.**

Rescuers Down Under: **FIND THE BOY.**

One Hundred and One Dalmatians:
SAVE THE PUPPIES.

Meet the Robinsons: **FIND MOM.**

The Team

Animation is a team sport. Yes, there are leaders and followers, but for the most part, a team of very creative people makes an animated film.

The **DIRECTOR** is the chief storyteller—the creative leader of a film. Directors guide the writers, actors, animators, and musicians toward the same vision so that they all tell the same story. The process of directing an animated film is a little like conducting a symphony orchestra. The director wants the best individual performance from each player, but also a great ensemble performance from the whole team. Though each individual artist on a movie works independently, they contribute to a single overall vision of the movie. The director keeps the vision on track and the team focused.

ABOVE: Joe Ranft's jaw-dropping sketch of Roger Rabbit's toon reaction; TOP: A design meeting with *Lilo & Stitch* producer Clark Spencer flanked by directors Dean DeBlois and Chris Sanders.

The **PRODUCER** is a team-builder, coach, psychotherapist, and cheerleader all wrapped into one. Producers have an important creative role in helping the directors tell the story by building a strong team of collaborators on each film. Yes, there are schedules and budgets to plan, but the producer's number one priority is to assemble and maintain a world-class team and create a movie of lasting quality. When people ask me what a producer does, my answer is deceptively simple: I hire the best people that I can find and then do exactly what they tell me to do.

WRITERS join a project early to develop the story idea in script form with the director. (It's not uncommon for a director to write his or her own script.) A script is a road map for a movie and the point of departure for any film project. In animation, it is a fluid document that changes as ideas grow and develop. Animation is a visual medium, so the writers work closely with story artists, visual development artists, and the director to create characters, dialogue, and situations that work well visually. It's a team effort that makes a story work, and a good writer is a crucial early collaborator.

ABOVE: Howard Ashman and Alan Menken brought their sizable talent to the development of *The Little Mermaid*, *Beauty and the Beast*, and *Aladdin*; BELOW: This deceptively simple Glen Keane *Tarzan* sketch suggests dynamic movement and camera angles, while showing the character's mood and determination.

If a film is a musical, it's time to fold **SONGWRITERS** into the process. Songs are everything in a true musical, because they are used to express the major turning points in the story. In fact, the story has to move ahead within the songs, or it will seem as if the movie has stopped dead just to give the characters a chance to sing. Songwriters come in very early during the storyboarding process to work with the director and "spot" moments in the story that could be musicalized. The songwriters create rough piano-and-vocal "demo" recordings of the songs. The story artists can board to these demos, and eventually the editor can cut these demos into the story reel with sketches to preview how each song is working. It's easy to make cuts and changes at this phase, as so little has been invested.

A **STORY ARTIST** is a unique talent who can both draw and tell a story. The work of the story crew starts at long story sessions, usually involving late nights and cold Chinese takeout. In this early phase, story artists explore situations that develop character personality, staging, comedy, or deep emotion. The early work is all about thinking and exploring. Ideas eventually take shape as drawings are pinned onto a storyboard, arranged so they can be read like a comic book. This early story phase is like feeling your way through a dark cave, blindfolded, with no flashlight. Any idea is welcome. There are no bad ideas at this point.

Simplicity and clarity are really important in storytelling. Once, my team and I pitched a complicated story idea to an executive, and after fifteen minutes, he stopped the meeting to ask, "Just tell me: what does this guy want and why can't he have it?" If you can answer that question, you have the beginning of a clear, strong story.

Like everyone working on an animated film, the story artist has to take whatever work the writer and visual development artists have done and continue to make it better. Walt Disney's artists use an odd word for this repetitive process: "plussing." Often, it means tossing out old or obsolete ideas in favor of better material. As a filmmaker, it hurts to cut out something that you love, but the brutal truth is that if it doesn't serve the story, it has to go. It's not bad to fail during this part of the process. In fact, if somebody told you that you would have a huge success only after you failed one hundred times, you'd want to fail as fast and often as possible so that you could work through all the bad material and get to the good stuff. So here are two important things to remember:

Writing is rewriting.
Fail fast, fail often.

9- 35.1

This watercolor is one of dozens that explored the look of the circus in *Dumbo* (1941).

Story Structure

There is a general structure that has evolved for most movies that divides a typical story into three acts. The first act introduces the characters and their world and then gets the character into some dilemma. It also clearly lays out the rules of the characters' world. For *Beauty and the Beast*, the first words you hear in the prologue contain the rules: "You must learn to love another and earn their love in return before the last petal falls. Then the spell will be broken." Act one ends

with a problem: Belle's father gets lost and is captured by Beast. Belle comes to rescue her father, and ends up taking his place. The curtain falls on act one.

The second act develops the plot to reveal the motives of the characters and the depth of their relationships. This act ends in a completely unsolvable problem for the hero, and all seems lost. Here are the beats (important points) of the second act of *Beauty and the Beast*:

ABOVE: A stained-glass window from the prologue of *Beauty and the Beast* foretells the brightness and darkness that is part of the Beast's story; OPPOSITE: Act two of *Beauty and the Beast* can be summed up simply in a short series of sketches.

Beast tries to befriend Belle, but also tells her not to go into the west wing.

The objects welcome Belle at dinner with "Be Our Guest."

After dinner, Belle wanders into the West Wing, and Beast scares her out of the castle.

Beast saves Belle from the wolves and they reach a quiet truce.

Gaston vows to have Belle as his wife by trapping Belle's father.

Beast and Belle fall in love, culminating in their ballroom dance.

On the balcony after the dance, Beast lets Belle go to her father, even though it means he will lose her and the spell will never be broken.

Belle returns home, but Gaston shows up with a crowd, ready to kill Beast.

Beast is heartbroken. All is lost *and* the bad guys are coming to kill him.

ABOVE: A strong moment of connection between Beast and Belle as shown in a simple Chris Sanders sketch; BELOW: The original story of *Lilo & Stitch* by Chris Sanders featured his character designs as part of the script; OPPOSITE: Art director Andy Gaskill and character designer Hans Bacher painted right on the script while exploring ideas for *Hercules.*

A tremendous character journey happens in this act. Belle goes from seeing Beast as a monster to seeing him as a loving friend. Though beginning as a pure animal, Beast soon reveals his inner love and humanity by first saving Belle, and then letting her go. Gaston doesn't know that Beast exists at the beginning of the act, but when he finds out, his plot line quickly escalates into a physical threat to kill Beast so he can have Belle for his own.

Act three is all about resolution. The characters enter the act in a hopeless situation.

The third act reveals their courage in the face of insurmountable odds, and often includes the undoing of evil, the triumph of the good, and the arrival "home" to a new psychological place.

In *Beauty and the Beast*, Beast fights and defeats Gaston, but after Belle shows up, Beast shows Gaston compassion and lets him go (safety tip: never turn your back on the villain). Belle and Beast are reunited, but Gaston jumps in and stabs Beast, before losing his footing and falling to his death. While Beast is dying in Belle's arms, the last rose petal falls. Once again, all seems lost, but the spell has been broken by Belle and Beast's love for each other, and the entire household transforms into humans again. Place happy ending here!

The three-act structure is only a guideline. It's important to be completely free with the story and let it be told in its own unique way.

STITCH

Intergalactic criminal. Wanted on twelve thousand counts of hooliganism, forgery, and repeated attempts to enslave planets. Strong. Ultra-intelligent. Bulletproof.

LILO
(LEE-LOW)

Five-year-old Polynesian girl. Lives with her older sister, Nani. Has a lot of trouble making friends due to an overactive and odd imagination. Eternally forgiving. Loves animals.

SIZE COMPARISON

INT. MUS/NIGHT

THIS MATERIAL IS THE
PROPERTY OF
THE WALT DISNEY COMPANY.
IT IS UNPUBLISHED AND
MAY NOT BE DUPLICATED
OR DISCLOSED TO UNAUTHORIZED
THIRD PARTIES, WITHOUT WRITTEN
PERMISSION FROM AN AUTHORIZED
OFFICER OF THE COMPANY.

CONFIDENTIAL

FADE IN:

INT. MUSEUM - NIGHT

We slowly TRUCK PAST imposing statues of ancient Greek Gods
and heroes, all dramatically lit. Offscreen NARRATION, a
dignified, resonant woman's voice, begins...

> VOICE (O.S.)
> Long ago, in the faraway land of
> ancient Greece, there was a
> golden age of powerful Gods and
> extraordinary heroes...

We TRUCK IN on a beautifully decorated vase depicting a
muscular figure wrestling a lion.

> VOICE (O.S., CONT.)
> And the greatest of all these
> heroes was the mighty Hercules,
> the strongest man who ever
> lived. Though of course, heroes
> must be measured not by the size
> of their strength, but by the
> strength of their hearts. Which
> brings us to the story we are
> about to...

The CAMERA HESITATES, looking for the source of the voice.

> VOICE (O.S., CONT.)
> We... are about to... AHEM!
> ...Down here!

The CAMERA ZIPS over to another vase, decorated with the
painted figures of five lovely WOMEN in long robes. As we
move in on the figures we see that one of them, CALLIOPE,
tall and regal, is alive. A moving illustration on the vase.
As she speaks, we realize the offscreen voice was hers.

> CALLIOPE (CONT.)
> Which brings us to the story we
> are about to tell. We are the
> Muses! Goddesses of the arts
> and proclaimers of heroes!
> Ladies!

The other women, come to life and turn toward Calliope.

> CALLIOPE (CONT.)
> Front and center! Names and
> specialties...

CGI ?

ZIP PAN TO

11.3A-002

Lilo:
"This is my room!"

11.3A-003

Lilo:
"This is your bed."

11.3A-004

STITCH: (ROWL)

11.3A-004

11.3A-005

Lilo:
"This is your dolly and bottle!"

11.3A-006

Lilo:
"See? Doesn't spill."

11.3A-007

I FILLED IT WITH COFFEE

11.3A-008

Lilo: GOOD PUPPY!
"Now get into bed!"
(sucks on bottle)

11.3A-009

LILO: "Augh!"

STITCH: "GRUNTS"

A Chris Sanders and Dean DeBlois storyboard from *Lilo & Stitch* combines sketches and dialogue strips to tell the story in the clearest, simplest way; OPPOSITE, CLOCKWISE FROM TOP LEFT: Walt Disney in a *Pinocchio* story meeting; Joe Ranft and John Lasseter hear a pitch for *Cars*; story artists sketch on digital tablets; brilliant story man Bill Peet boarded *The Jungle Book* and *One Hundred and One Dalmatians* nearly by himself.

The Pitch

When all the writing and drawing is done, it comes time to pitch the storyboards to the director and the story crew. A storyboard pitch is acting, storytelling, and salesmanship all rolled into one. The story artist stands in front of the storyboards with a pointer and walks through the scene, sketch by sketch. If the sequence isn't working here, it isn't going to work in the film.

Up until recently, artists would pin their story sketches to a four-foot-by-eight-foot board so the sequence could be pitched in comic-strip fashion and discussed in a story meeting. Now, most story artists draw on a digital tablet and make their pitch either by showing one sketch at a time on a screen, or by formatting their sketches into a simple digital slideshow with temporary dialogue to help them with the pitch process.

Here's where the story artist needs the patience and persistence of a gold miner. The typical sequence goes through a lot (and I mean *a lot*) of corrections, redraws, rethinks, throw-outs, and re-dos until the scene works perfectly for the director. All this will change *again* when the work gets edited into a "story reel" with dialogue and effects. What works on the written page doesn't necessarily work when it's drawn. What works on a storyboard doesn't necessarily work when it's put up on a movie screen with dialogue. This process of making the film better at each turn is grueling, but it almost always yields the best movie for the audience.

Put It Together, Take It Apart

ABOVE LEFT: The *Atlantis* production team gathers in a story room to pitch and discuss ideas; ABOVE RIGHT: The editor pulls together thousands of sketches and recorded lines of dialogue on a non-linear computer-based editing system.

An **EDITOR** joins the team now, becoming probably the closest collaborator to the director through the remaining process of filmmaking. When a sequence of story sketches is ready to be turned over to the editor, the story team meets to pitch the finished storyboard in detail, describing camera moves, sound effects, music ideas, and anything else that might help tell the story.

Editors use a computer to assemble the story sketches into a timeline, representing the continuity of the story as it was originally envisioned on the storyboards. Temporary dialogue (sometimes called "scratch dialogue") gets recorded by stand-in actors or even by animators, story artists, the coffee guy, and pretty much anybody else in the studio who can act. This gives the director and editor a

preliminary sense of the performance and pacing for the scene, acting as a trial run for the dialogue before the final actors are brought in to record.

Dozens of tracks of dialogue, music, and sound effects can be added into the editor's computer timeline in sync with the picture to form a good working version of any given sequence. This rough assembly is called the story reel (also sometimes called a work reel, show reel, animatic, or Leica reel).

The editorial crew keeps track of a million picture, music, and sound details. Each sequence is constantly polished and "plussed" with revised dialogue and sketches. When one sequence is complete, it is joined with other sequences to form a finished act. Eventually, when all three acts are done, they are joined together to form a complete rough cut of the movie. This first version of the film is really rough—sometimes embarrassingly rough and difficult to sit through. Then the real process of "plussing" in animation kicks in once again.

It is an iterative process that goes something like this:

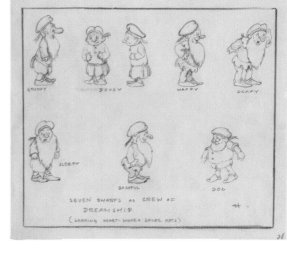

➤ **Screen it.**

➤ **Discuss it.**

➤ **Get that sinking feeling that you don't know what you're doing.**

➤ **Weep openly.**

➤ **Tear it apart.**

➤ **Correct it.**

➤ **Re-board it.**

➤ **Rebuild it.**

➤ **Screen it again.**

➤ **Repeat as necessary.**

It takes five or six trips through this process of building and rebuilding before the film is working well enough to go into any sort of production. Entire sequences get cut. Entire characters get cut. And under extreme conditions, the entire movie gets shelved.

An editor holds a crucial job: to always stay objective during the making of a film and suggest cuts or re-ordering of material to help the story's flow. Editors also drive the post-production process when the film is near completion. More on that later.

TOP: Some dwarfs didn't make it into the film; ABOVE LEFT, CENTER, AND RIGHT: These characters were developed for a film called *Wild Life*. The entire film was shelved; LEFT: Rocky the Rhino was completely cut out of *The Jungle Book*; FOLLOWING PAGES: Designer Kay Nielsen and his assistant Bill Wallett's stunning sketches in colored crayon and gouache for a *Fantasia* sequence based on Wagner's "Ride of the Valkyries." The sequence was never produced.

Design

A **PRODUCTION DESIGNER** is responsible for the way a movie looks. Everything that you see on the screen has been thought about, debated, and designed with the guidance of the production designer. On many animated films, the production designer creates the overarching design of the film and then works with an **ART DIRECTOR** who sees that the design is executed through every frame.

The production designer, art director, and their team create a whole new world on the screen—a world that will transport the audience and help tell the story.

For *The Incredibles*, Teddy Newton did hundreds of exploratory pieces to help define the world of the film. His work in collage or paint is strong, graphic, sometimes abstract, but always inspirational. At this point, it's not important

ABOVE AND LEFT: Teddy Newton's design explorations for *The Incredibles*; BELOW: A visual development painting of *Bolt* by art director Paul Felix; BOTTOM LEFT: A final frame from Eric Goldberg's "Rhapsody in Blue" sequence from *Fantasia 2000*.

that each designer capture exactly what the final film will look like. The spirit of the film and its color-and-design vocabulary are more important. The definitive final style will be ironed out soon enough, but now is the time to dream and push all the design aspects of the film to their limits.

ABOVE: This visual development painting sets the style for the upcoming film *Rapunzel*; ABOVE RIGHT: A dynamic action sketch by Aaron Blaise from *Brother Bear*; BELOW: a color idea for Rafiki's tree from *The Lion King*.

VISUAL DEVELOPMENT ARTISTS form part of a film's art direction team. Their job is to create art that helps explore and visualize the universe of the film and to take an early try at illustrating specific moments in the story. Sometimes their work is executed in a simple sketch. Other times it is a breathtaking painting that suggests a final frame of the film. Sometimes they will even devise a "motion test," which shows the potential of the camera moving through a location. Visual development art grows out of the script and the storyboards, but "viz dev" artists also create pieces not in the script that might inspire new visual ideas. It's their job to play with the endless imaginative possibilities of visual storytelling.

A character designer has to put a face on a personality. The story is about characters—their hopes and dreams, their weaknesses and vulnerabilities. A designer has to completely understand those character traits and then search for ways to capture that personality on a piece of paper. Some people make the fatal mistake of designing a character from the outside in. Yes, you can draw a cute mouse or an evil-looking bad guy, but those drawings have nothing to do with storytelling or personality. Building a character from the inside out is much more in tune with "personality animation." Great character designers start with the internal elements that motivate a character, and then start to draw around those personality traits, eventually breathing life into a character that is completely believable in every way.

First and foremost, a character has to be appealing to the audience. Appeal is a subjective thing that doesn't just extend to cute bunnies and pretty princesses. Every character needs its own "watchability"—that certain something that makes you want to follow the character no matter what. There's an appealing quality to Cruella De Vil or Gaston although they're villains. The comedic characters Mr. Potato Head and Goofy are very appealing. Even props and sets need an appeal that entices the audience to look more closely.

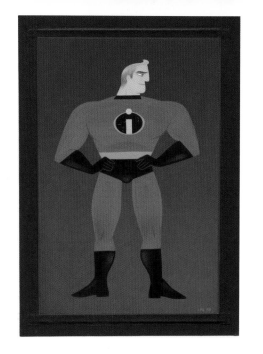

Once the basic ensemble of characters is roughed out, the designer starts to play with the costume changes needed to tell the story. In *The Incredibles*, costumes help change a normal family into a family of superheroes. In *Mulan*, the lead character transforms from beautiful young girl to brave male warrior and back again. That's a challenge.

The costume designs, fabrics, and colors of a character are important as indicators of personality, too. It's especially true in a CG film where costume and fabric selection can tell a lot about the social standing and personal style of the character. As the old saying goes: clothes make the 'toon. The biggest test comes when the character (whether drawn or built in a computer) gets into the hands of the animator. Animators put the character through some preliminary calisthenics to make sure the design works. If the character is awkward to move or doesn't look right from certain angles, it's back to the drawing board until the animator can make the character perform in any situation.

The final important design consideration involves putting all the characters together, side by side, to check their shapes and silhouettes as an ensemble. The audience needs to know clearly at a glance who each character is. Think of Mike and Sulley in *Monsters, Inc.* They have immediately recognizable designs built around a simple green circle and a blue rectangle.

OPPOSITE: Designers use any style and any medium to search for an effective character and costume design; TOP: A lineup of characters from *Alice in Wonderland*, used to check for variety of shape and size; ABOVE RIGHT: Costume sketch by Chen-Yi Chang for *Mulan*; RIGHT: A Pixar artist sculpting the Mr. Incredible maquette.

In the 1930s, Walt Disney formed a model department that sculpted characters as a part of the character-design process. The sculptures, called "maquettes," let the crew see and study the proportions of a character and the textures of costume in three dimensions. Even now, **SCULPTORS** are very much a part of the design process. Final sculptures can be digitized into the computer for CG modelers to use, or used by CG lighters before they dive into the computer to see how the form of the character behaves under lights in three dimensions. In a CG film, a maquette can be sculpted after a character is modeled in the computer. A digital lathe reads the information on the shape of the character and carves out the form in resin as an exact replica of the digital model. For a 2-D film, the maquette is an invaluable tool used by animators and their assistants to see the character from every hard-to-draw angle. And finally, in a stop-motion movie, the sculptures are literally used in the creation of the puppets that appear on the screen.

Voices

After the filmmakers have developed characters to tell their story, the search begins for the voices that will bring those characters to life. The voice needs to be a perfect companion for the design of the character. In fact, after preliminary design drawings are done, it's not unusual for the look of a character to change a little when the voice is cast. Voices provide very specific clues to personality. The attitude, behavior, emotional response, and individual character traits of an actor inspire an animator to create a nuanced personality. There are exceptions, of course—for example, Dumbo or Dopey, who don't speak—but when the marriage of actor and design come together, it's magic. It's hard to imagine Mrs. Potts without the voice of Angela Lansbury, or Buzz and Woody without the contributions of Tim Allen and Tom Hanks.

Voices need to work as an ensemble. If you listen to the whole cast with your eyes closed, the range of voices can be quite different. Like singers, some voices are a high soprano or a tenor range, whereas others are low and resonant. This range of voice tone is important and gives audio diversity to the ensemble cast.

Once the **VOICE ACTORS** are cast, they come into a recording studio to record their lines of dialogue. The voice actors are recorded early, before any animation is fully finished, as their delivery, timing, and attitude will inspire the animators. An actor will continue to record many times over the course of a movie. As with everything in animation, it's an iterative process.

With each session, new sequences of the movie are recorded along with rewrites on dialogue from previous recording sessions. The director works with the actor on each line, sometimes repeating an individual line many many times until it's just what the director is looking for.

The director works with the editor to assemble the best takes from each actor into a sort of "radio show" to hear how the dialogue and voices interact. The original rough scratch dialogue is tossed, and the final takes of each vocal performance are assembled into a new dialogue track. Story sketches, sound effects, and music are added into the story reel, which allows the filmmakers to evaluate how the story is shaping up with the final vocal performances inserted.

FAR LEFT: *The Jungle Book* director Woolie Reitherman coaches his son Bruce, the voice of Mowgli; LEFT: John Lasseter records dialogue for *Cars* with Pixar favorite John Ratzenberger; OPPOSITE: A partial look at the cast of voices and characters for *Cars*.

SARGE
PAUL DOOLEY

FILLMORE
GEORGE CARLIN

DOC HUDSON
PAUL NEWMAN

MATER
LARRY THE CABLE GUY

SALLY
BONNIE HUNT

LIGHTNING
MCQUEEN
OWEN WILSON

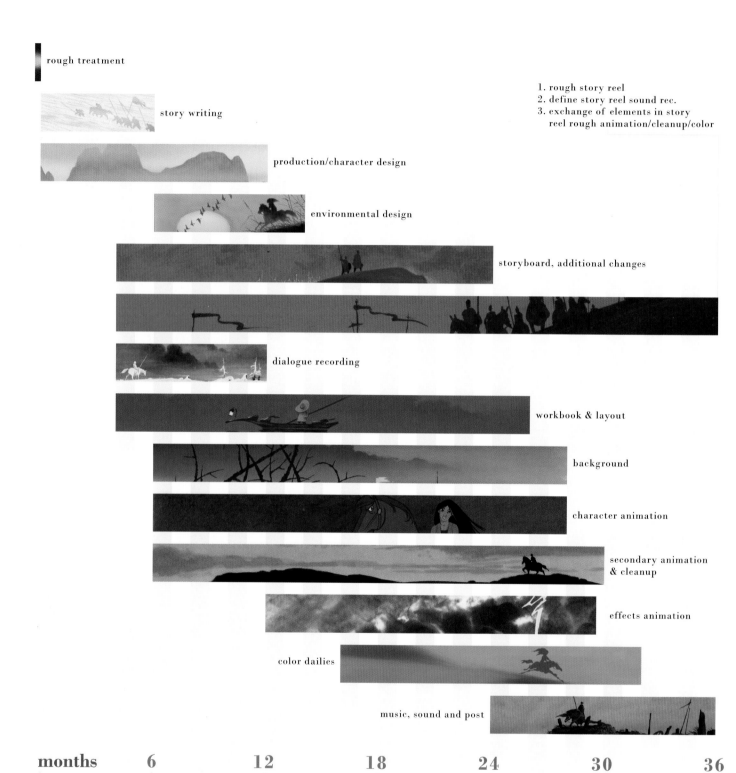

rough treatment

story writing

1. rough story reel
2. define story reel sound rec.
3. exchange of elements in story
   reel rough animation/cleanup/color

production/character design

environmental design

storyboard, additional changes

dialogue recording

workbook & layout

background

character animation

secondary animation
& cleanup

effects animation

color dailies

music, sound and post

months   6   12   18   24   30   36

The Production Team

The **ASSOCIATE PRODUCER** has three things (three *big* things) to worry about: people, time, and money. Associate producers are always solving problems that sound like they come from some nightmarish math test. For example:

> *If an animator can complete four seconds of film per week, and the film is ninety minutes long and has to be animated in fifty-two weeks, how many animators will you need to complete the film on time?*

You can figure out the mathematical answer (twenty-six), but the real answer depends on how many characters there are per second; how experienced the animators are; how many holidays, sick days, and vacation days fall in that year; how much overtime the budget allows; how many versions are required before the scene gets approved; and how many computer crashes will take place during that fifty-two weeks. The art of producing and managing an animated movie also has to allow for false starts, changes, and animation that doesn't work the first time around.

Being a **PRODUCTION MANAGER (PM)** for an animated film is like being the mayor of a small city full of filmmakers. The PM works closely with the producers to set goals for each week and manage the daily flow of work. Each department will need director time, critique sessions need to be scheduled, and regular production meetings need to be called in order to keep information flowing between departments.

The entire film crew is grouped by department, and each department has a **DEPARTMENT HEAD** who is a senior artist or technician that manages the artistic or technical goals of a particular department. Most important, the department head keeps watch over the quality level of the work, be it animation, modeling, or visual effects.

The department runs like a small business. A **PRODUCTION DEPARTMENT MANAGER (PDM)** (some studios call them assistant production managers or production co-coordinators) runs the department's business. PDMs report to the production manager and work as a team with other PDMs to manage the production each week. Then there are armies of tireless production secretaries, production assistants, and administrative staff that do everything from typing scripts and memos to arranging for catering during the production crunch, answering phones, booking travel, scheduling massages for tired artists, making coffee, running errands, and generally helping to move the production ahead.

You'll notice that, up until now, the early development of a film is pretty much the same whether it is computer-generated, hand-drawn, or stop-motion animation. Buckle your seat belts, because here's where the changes of animation technique start to show up. Each technique has strengths and weaknesses and each has its own charm and appeal. It's up to the director and the creative team to decide which technique will be best for their particular story.

OPPOSITE: Work on an animated film passes through a series of departments, from initial story to final post production. The work flows through a "production pipeline" that is carefully scheduled to meet the release date of the film. Here's a schedule for a typical 2-D animated film to be produced over three years—most of the time this process takes even longer.

Story sketch from *Peter Pan*.

ACT TWO

The Creation

Here's where our journey to the movie screen breaks off, as we explore three different animation techniques. The production process for the computer-generated *Finding Nemo* is very different from that for the hand-drawn *Little Mermaid*, and both are vastly different from the production process for the stop-motion film *Tim Burton's The Nightmare Before Christmas*. Here is a look at all three techniques.

ABOVE: *Fantasia* story sketch; TOP LEFT: Story time with Walt Disney and his crew; TOP RIGHT: An early Bud Luckey sketch of Buzz Lightyear; RIGHT: Final frame from *Finding Nemo*; OPPOSITE, CLOCKWISE FROM TOP LEFT: An early Joe Grant sketch for *Dumbo*; final frame from *The Nightmare Before Christmas*; a Tim Burton sketch for *Frankenweenie*; final frame from *The Little Mermaid*; FOLLOWING PAGES: A stunning visual development piece from *Wall-E*.

"Art challenges technology, and technology inspires the art." —*John Lasseter*

Computer- Generated Production

My daughter's school has a black-box theater. It is a completely empty black room with four walls, a floor, and a ceiling. That's it. Now imagine putting on a play in this black-box theater where there are no sets, lights, props, or actors. This is how a computer-generated (CG) animated film starts. Everything in the black box—in this case, the virtual world inside a computer—needs to be designed and built to be able to put on a show.

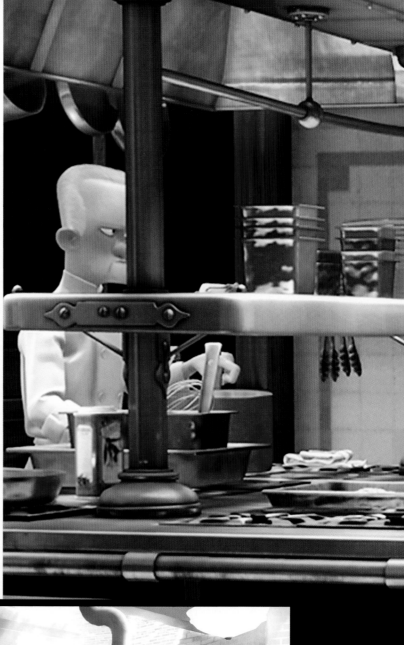

BELOW: An early idea for the kitchen in *Ratatouille* is stunningly realized in the final film (RIGHT).

KITCHEN

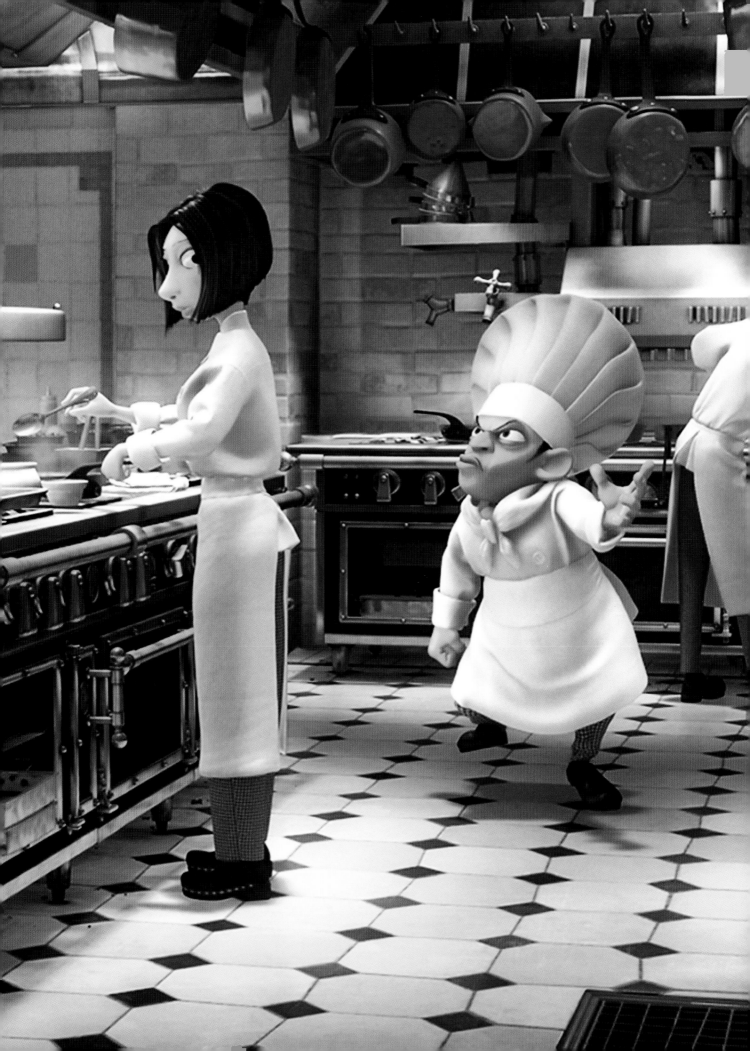

Building the World

In pre-production, the production designer and art director create a look for the film as well as commissioning probably thousands of drawings and paintings that define that look. Next, it's time to turn those designs into virtual film sets. Artists called **MODELERS** are the "builders" on a CG movie. Working closely with the production designer, modelers build the elaborate sets and props for a film using software tools specially made for the job. The sets have to serve the action of the movie and the demands of the story, but most important, they have to reveal something about the characters that inhabit these spaces, so the details of the set-dressing and props in a room are crucial. Here's where research gives the crew a foundation of knowledge to build on. The artists on *Ratatouille* visited dozens of restaurant kitchens in Paris. The *Cars* crew took a cross-country trip along Route 66 to experience roadside culture. The crew of *A Bug's Life* even got down on the ground with their magnifying glasses to study a bug's-eye view of the real world. Books, photos, films, field trips, and Web-based research also help ground the set designs in a plausible world. (Please don't confuse "plausible" with "realistic." The world of an animated film is never meant to be reality, but rather a caricature of reality.)

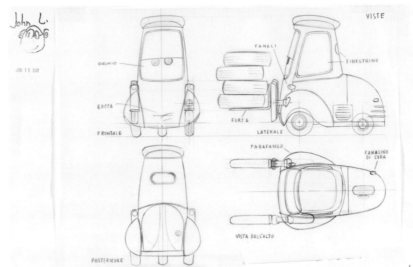

ABOVE and **BELOW:** Guido takes shape from early sketches to the final character. **OPPOSITE:** An incredibly detailed map of Radiator Springs helped designers and modelers construct the town. Story inspires the look and function of the town.

Hopper Wing Study —

Outstretched
Wings

Resting Position

color splotching
evident in Hopper a[...]

Hopper Wing

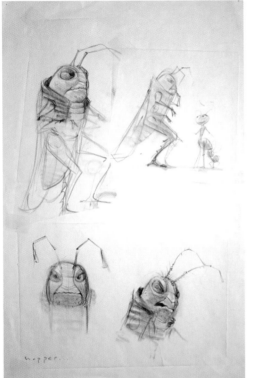

hopper

ABOVE and LEFT: A
modeler's collection of
references to build Hopper
from *A Bug's Life*. Modelers
build the characters while
always aware that the
forms of the character will
be merged with surface
colors and textures.

Sets are built with varying degrees of detail. A space such as the inside of Mr. Incredible's house uses a very detailed model. As you look out the window at neighborhood streets and trees, the model will have less detail, and distant hills or sky might be a scenic backdrop painted on a big virtual billboard. The level of detail in a set is determined by where the action takes place, and modelers simplify detail the further it is from the focal point of a scene to save building and computing time.

Modelers also tackle one of the most demanding jobs on a movie: modeling the characters. All the pre-production designs for the characters and their costume changes arrive on the modeler's desktop. Bit by bit, the modeler uses a set of digital tools to sculpt a three-dimensional digital model of the character in space. Instead of clay, the modeler uses bits of geometry of every shape and size called polygons to piece together a character model. When it's finished, the polygon version of a character looks like a wire-frame birdcage. Later, the surfaces will be "skinned," and textures will be deployed to finish the look of the character.

Many character models contain invisible "bones" and "muscles" inside; this helps the character maintain a naturalistic anatomy when it's moved by the animator. The modeler also has to be aware of the final look of the character. Costumes, clothes, hair, and fur have to be planned for, but for now, the model looks more like a gray marionette, with no colors, textures, or strings attached.

A **RIGGER** takes a modeled character and attaches the animation controls that will allow an animator to move the model around, much as a puppeteer uses strings to manipulate a marionette. The rigger's controls need to move every bit of the character. Unlike strings on a marionette, these "strings" are invisible and highly sensitive, and there are a lot of them. For example, an arm needs controls for the shoulder, elbow, and wrist joints plus more controls to move each finger and the thumb. Each joint has to move and rotate like a real arm, while still giving the animator enough flexibility to stretch, squash, pull, and distort the arm if the action calls for it.

The muscle and bone under the arm will help define the movement of the skin, but the rigger also has to give the animator controls for hair, clothes, fur, and feathers.

A CG character must look good from every angle, in every conceivable movement; so before any animation begins, the rigger and the animator work closely to create a set of "rig calisthenics" to "exercise" the character through its paces and find out where any problems are. Little things, like crinkles and creases at elbows and joints, need to be fixed. The rig has to perform the character's subtle facial articulation over a broad range of dialogue and emotion, so the face is the center of hundreds of controls with which the animator can execute the most nuanced expressions. To make the rigger's life easier, multiple controls are often batched together into a single control that moves several related body parts at once.

THIS PAGE: Buck Cluck is modeled from sketches and isometric drawings of the character. The final model (FAR RIGHT) lacks texture and color, which will be added later in look development. After the model was rigged for movement, the *Chicken Little* animators used a proprietary tool called "shelf control" (NEAR RIGHT) to isolate and move parts of the character.

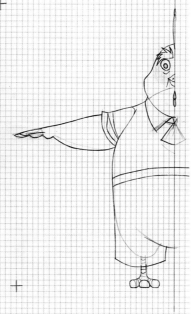
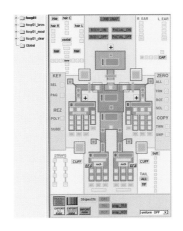

Cinematography

THESE PAGES: *Mulan* production designer Hans Bacher does hundreds of studies to explore ideas for staging and camera placement. His studies use a strong composition of light and shadow to direct the audience to the subject of the scene.

A movie screen is a simple, white rectangle. That rectangle is the audience's "window" into the movie. A **CINEMATOGRAPHER** works with the director to plan exactly what the audience sees through that window, up on the movie screen. Cinematographers use the tools of cinema—composition, lighting, color, movement—to tell the story. Every live-action film has a cinematographer, but the job is fairly new to animation, and more and more animated films are hiring dedicated cinematographers to be part of the creative team.

The **LAYOUT ARTIST** designs and creates the film sets; the stages for the animated characters to act on. The sets, dozens of them in each film, will reveal elements of character and story, but must also create visual interest and an illusion of depth on the flat, white movie screen. After the sets are built, the layout artist tackles the scene-to-scene planning of each sequence with the cinematographer in a process called "pre-viz" (short for pre-visualization). Using simplified, low-polygon CG character stand-ins, the team can go through a sequence in the film and decide camera angles, camera movement, and blocking (placement of the actors in the scene). It's the first time that the director can get a feeling for how the characters look and feel on the set. This step is a very crude rehearsal compared to the final film, but as with most things in animation, you start simple, then layer levels of detail and complexity until the shot is done.

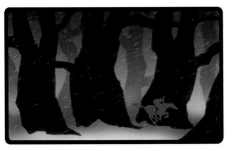

THE ALCHEMY OF ANIMATION

THESE PAGES: Three-dimensional layout panels from *Bolt* portray cinematography for an action packed sequence; ABOVE: Final frame from *Bolt*.

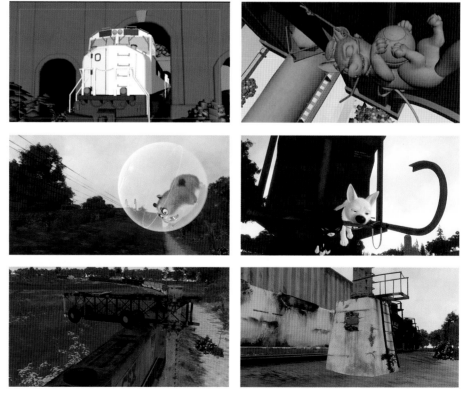

Art and Technology

A **TECHNICAL DIRECTOR (TD)** is a highly creative jack-of-all-trades who is part artist, part technician. TDs work with the crew at nearly every step of production to solve problems, participate in designs, create smooth work flow, and bridge the gap between artistic vision and technical solution. A great TD not only has strong technical skills, but also artistic experience—along with a healthy dose of common sense.

The job starts with making sure the artists have user-friendly computer screens to work on. For example, the artist sees only a "user interface," a control panel that lets the animator move the rigged character (or rig). If the interface is too complicated or poorly designed, it can make the animator's job impossible, like working with oven mitts on your hands.

Just think of all the elements that can go into one shot in a film—camera movement, props, hair, fur, clothing, special effects, and lighting. The TD has to work with and support all the departments from design and modeling to animation, lighting, effects, and rendering to make sure the work flows smoothly down the production pipeline. This requires knowledge of tools and software, the ability to solve problems, and the support of many individual artists on the film.

Examples of just three of the many stages of the look development process. In this case, an initial pass defines surface textures (TOP LEFT); gray cards represent where individual feather paintings will be placed (LEFT); and final look development (ABOVE).

story really well. But *Monsters, Inc.*, needed one of the main characters, Sulley, to be completely covered in fur from head to toe. At the time, you couldn't just go to the store and buy software to do this, so the software crew wrote tools to grow and groom fur on a computer-generated character. They also created other tools and procedures to manipulate that fur in just about any way that an artist might need. It was a huge breakthrough.

The software team doesn't develop their tools in a vacuum. The close and equal collaboration of technical and artistic filmmakers produces the best circumstances for quality and yields the best software tools to fit the needs of the story. Always remember that everybody tells the story—everybody, even the software developer.

LEFT: The original design sketch for Mike and Sulley by Peter Docter was as elegantly simple as a circle and a rectangle. Even though the final characters are built and textured in a very sophisticated way, that simple circle and rectangle still underlie the final characters (BELOW).

CG filmmakers can purchase computer software that does a lot of their work for them, but there are some things that normal off-the-shelf software can't do. That's where a **SOFTWARE DEVELOPER** steps in. This is a person constantly trying out new software packages and testing new commercially available tools. Each film is different, so if a project needs a particular tool that doesn't exist, a software engineer can create a custom tool for that production.

Here's an example of tool design and development: the CG characters from *Toy Story* looked solid and made from plastic, which fit the

LOOK DEVELOPMENT ARTISTS use a variety of tools to create the look of the surfaces on the character. Some look development artists are painters, whereas others are programmers. The artists add colors and textures to the character to help determine how it reacts to light. Fabric, fur, skin, hair, or shiny surfaces such as plastic or chrome are developed by the "Look Dev" team and then tested on the character. Subtle adjustments are made to get the exact look of how light is absorbed, reflected, or internally scattered by the form of the character. Human skin, for example, can look pretty flat and plastic unless artists deploy subsurface scattering techniques to simulate the complex way that light interacts with different layers of skin. The same technique could be used on something as different as a marble surface to create a more realistic look.

Look development artists use three-dimensional paintbrushes, software procedures, and "texture maps" that wrap a texture around an object. Texture maps are similar to gift-wrapping—wrap a box with a wood texture, and it looks like a box made from wood. Wrap it with a pink plastic texture, and it looks like a pink plastic box. There are also "bump maps" or "displacement maps" that can create minor elevations or depressions on a surface. A program called a "shader" interprets how to apply the texture and how the texture reacts to light. The definition of the term "shader" has evolved and expanded over time; a shader now applies more broadly to how the different inputs (textures, fur parameters, bumps, displacements, etc.) all blend with lighting to give the character or object its final appearance.

Final frame from the Pixar short *Lifted.*

Creating Life

The set is built and the lights are in place. The characters and props have been designed and rigged, and the tools are all set. Now, the animator is ready to work.

ANIMATORS are like actors: they need to prepare for their performance in many ways. First, they soak up all the research and inspirational art. They study the storyboards, the vocal performances, and the story objective of the scene. Then, before work starts on a

animators are stronger with comedy, some with subtle emotion, some with drama and power. Next, more tests, more adjustments, and more practice swings happen, so mistakes are caught before the work begins on production.

Veteran Disney animator Eric Larson always summed up the goals of personality animation in one word: sincerity. But the process of putting a real, sincere, living performance on the screen using only pixels is not easy.

OPPOSITE: Animation of the Bowler Hat Guy from *Meet the Robinsons* was very broad and deliberate; ABOVE: Animation breakdown of Chicken Little break-dancing.

production scene, they play with some experimental animation to make sure that they are completely comfortable with the character rig. It's a little like a golfer taking a practice swing.

With all the research complete, the animator will go over the scene at length with the director, making thumbnail sketches or acting out everything about the scene so the assignment is really clear. The director usually casts animators on specific characters to take advantage of their acting strengths. As is true of actors, some

Animators start by posing the character into several of the most extreme movements in a given scene. When strung together, these extremes, or "key frames," form the basic action pattern for the scene. Between each of these key frames, the animator will start to break down and time out the action even more. If the scene lasts for five seconds, the animator plays with the timing of the character over those five seconds, using the computer to help create the frames "in-between" his key frames to fill out the movement.

In 2006, Ollie Johnston, the last of Walt's famous "Nine Old Men," visited Pixar. Eager to show him our methods, animators demonstrated Pixar's software, explaining how key poses and splines were created. Early in the demonstration, Ollie raised his hands. "Wait, wait, wait," he said, "What happens first?" Animators explained that they acted out or thumbnailed their scenes. Ollie shook his head. "Yes, but what happens first?" Animators looked at each other, and replied, "Well, we think about what the character is thinking and assign poses to express each thought." Ollie nodded his head, smiling. "That's what I wanted to hear."

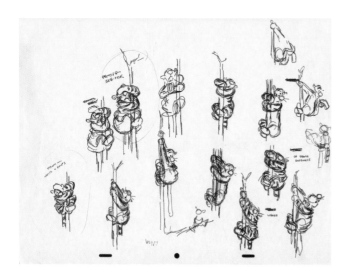

ABOVE: Thumbnails of Tigger show the complete planning and thought before a scene begins; BELOW: Pixar animator Victor Navone worked out his animation of Dash in a series of stick figures before approaching the computer to work.

A 3-D animator's art is complex. Here are four steps that I think describe the principles of character animation and provide a process for animating a scene:

THINK

➤ **What is the purpose of this scene in the movie?**

➤ **What is the most entertaining way to show the action?**

➤ **What is the character thinking and feeling?**

➤ **Where is this in the plot?**

➤ **Why am I here? I can't do this.**

ABOVE: Milt Kahl sketched dozens of thumbnails before he started animating a scene of Madame Medusa.

PLAN

➤ Visualize the scene in your head first; animate last.

➤ Act out the scene . . . what does it feel like physically?

➤ How does the scene connect with the shots before it or after it?

➤ Do you understand the layout, set design, prop location, and proposed camera moves?

➤ Do you know the overall mood, lighting, and time of day?

➤ What is the emotion in this scene?

➤ What are the subtleties of emotion in the vocal performance and dialogue?

➤ Plan out all the patterns of movement with thumbnail sketches.

➤ Talk the idea over with the director to make sure all agree.

➤ Stock up on coffee, close your door, and go to work.

RIGHT AND BELOW: It can be very difficult in CG to make interaction between characters believable, not only with hands but also with the eyes. Action analysis and strong tools let the animator break this barrier and allow characters to perform in a very tactile way.

ANIMATE

➤ Strive for the most effective and clearest extreme poses.

➤ Where do you want the audience to look?

➤ What is the rhythm of this scene (fast vs. slow, kinetic vs. restful)?

➤ Don't move anything without a purpose. Holding still is just as important as moving.

➤ Let the whole character tell the story, not just the eyes or head.

➤ Don't be lazy and let the computer do the work. Computers don't animate, people do. If the computer software creates a timing or movement that you don't like, don't accept it. Get in and change it until it's right.

➤ Think clarity. Could you follow what's happening in the scene even if the character were in silhouette?

➤ Don't just illustrate dialogue; illustrate emotions, thoughts, and ideas.

➤ Simplify dialogue into phrases, and illustrate the dominant vowel and consonant sounds, especially for fast dialogue. (We don't flap our whole mouth with every word of dialogue. We phrase our speech into simple, economical patterns of movement.)

➤ Changes of expression are major points of interest to the audience. Make sure the expression is clearly visible and that it reads clearly as it changes.

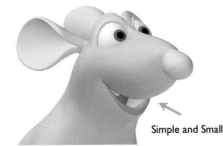

Simple and Small

Busy and Large

"PLUS" IT

➤ **Don't fall in love with your first effort. Revisit your scene and look again.**

➤ **Simplify, simplify, simplify: most new animators move the character too much without letting the character think, absorb, and reflect. Be critical and edit out movement that doesn't contribute to the performance.**

➤ **Look at the secondary actions in a scene (overlapping fabric, hair). Do they contribute to the idea of the scene or just distract from it?**

➤ **Is the character alive? Animation is not about movement, it's about life. Breathe life into a scene both visually and emotionally.**

➤ **Look again at clarity of communication. The audience only has one twenty-fourth of a second to read an individual frame of animation, so it has to read really clearly.**

➤ **Don't hide. Animation is a team sport. Show your work to the director and other animators and listen to their reaction. It doesn't mean you have to make every change they recommend, but fresh eyes always help to plus a scene.**

ABOVE: Mr. Incredible demonstrates "squash" and "stretch;" TOP AND BOTTOM: Creating appeal in rats was no small task. Silhouettes were kept as very simple shapes. Mouths were kept simple and small, and the relationship between Remy's mouth, cheeks, eyes, and ears was carefully designed and animated to keep him appealing despite his rodent lineage.

After the primary animation is complete, animators collaborate with character TDs to set up simulations for fabric, fur, and hair. These simulations account for weight, gravity, and even collisions between a garment and its surroundings. Animators can add virtual wind to make the character look like its hair is blowing in the breeze. The simulation won't be perfect every time, so the animator can alter the timing by changing the passage of time or by digitally "clothespinning" fabric to make it stay still.

YES   NO

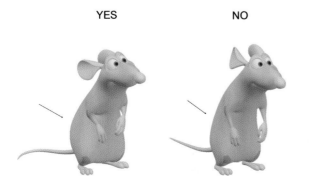

RIGHT: Walt Disney studies a film test on his Moviola (circa 1940). Today, the same test scene is viewed as a digital image on a computer screen; OPPOSITE: The final scenes of the Oscar-nominated short *The Little Matchgirl* were done first without the little girl's body and then with the girl added but covered with too much snow. Finally by using the girl and less snow, and pulling the camera back further, the scene worked. Each version had an emotional affect on the outcome of the film.

Sweatbox: The Peer Review

"Sweatbox" is the term used to describe a meeting between the director and the animators to critique individual scenes of a film. This odd-sounding expression was inspired by Walt Disney's own small screening room at his Hyperion studio, which didn't have air conditioning.

This is the ultimate peer review, where the director and crew can talk with complete honesty about the animation, effects, layout, and camera movement of a scene before it is put into final color. Sweatboxing happens at regular intervals throughout the making of a film. Each step of the way, the director views

and okays each individual shot. The sessions are pretty dynamic—and brutally honest. Honest, tough criticism makes each scene as good as it can be, and everyone in the room gets to see where the director is setting the bar for quality and entertainment. Everyone is watching for mistakes or trying to find ways to "plus" the scene. As each scene is animated, the director approves the shot to move on to the next step, culminating with putting it in color. As each final color shot is cut into the reel piece by piece, the film gradually becomes finished—like an elaborate puzzle coming together one piece at a time.

THE ALCHEMY OF ANIMATION

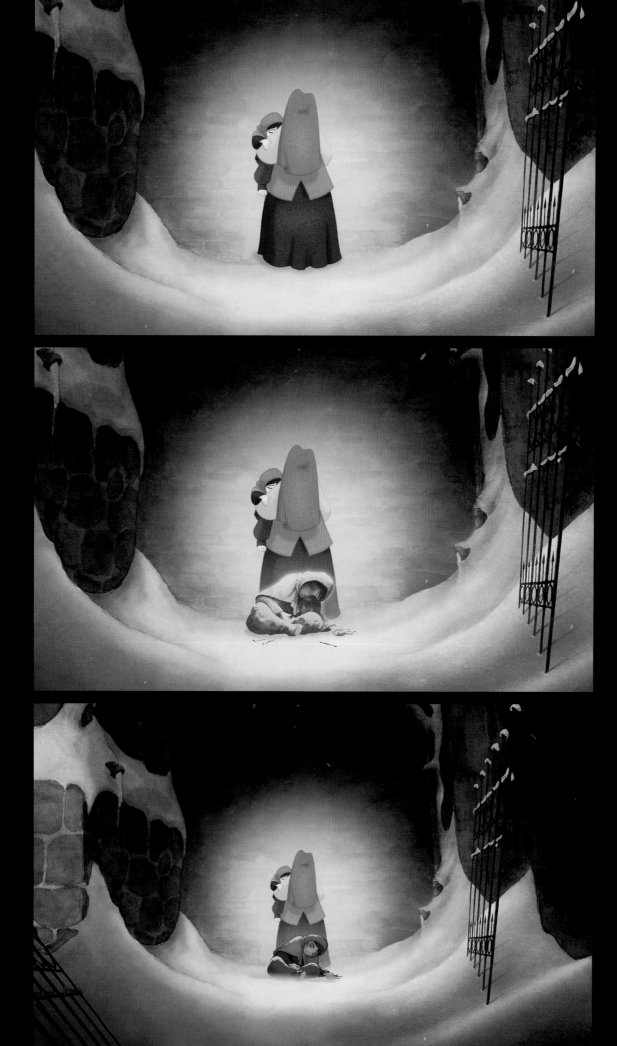

Visual Effects

ABOVE: Even the most subtle effects, such as the texture of this dough from a kitchen scene in *Ratatouille*, have to be accounted for.

Our story may be about characters and their journeys, but it's also about how the forces of nature act on their world. Wind, rain, sunlight, mist, fog, shadows, and fire are all the domain of the **VISUAL EFFECTS ANIMATOR**, who helps to create the feeling of a believable, plausible environment.

Visual effects artists are unique: they are fascinated by the world of both natural and extremely *un*natural phenomena. Unlike their counterparts in character animation, they probably grew up interested in magic, explosions, and laser blasts, rather than bunnies or bears.

Although a film may call for a huge thunderstorm or some other large visual effects set piece, even the smallest scenes usually contain a visual effects component that an effects animator will need to evaluate and solve. Each individual effect needs a unique approach. Sometimes it's as easy as grabbing an existing software package to create the look, but a large part of this job is researching or developing new cutting-edge tools to create an effect or solve a visual problem.

Each film presents challenges. The effects animators and TDs start by studying the

demands of the story. For example, Mark Dindal, the director of *Chicken Little*, created an elaborate sequence with characters being chased through a cornfield by aliens.

The effects team went to work developing a "cornfield tool" and a work flow pipeline to handle the animation of thousands of stalks of corn. The stalks had to react as the characters ran past, but they also had to blow in the wind and be chopped to pieces by aliens. The digital pipeline needed to be robust enough to handle the data created by tens of thousands of corn stalks—each moving independently and reacting to the needs of the scene—yet simple enough to be manipulated by the most non-technical artist working on the movie.

The team developed a tool to create cycles of movement that made thousands of stalks of corn shake, straighten, or bend in the wind. They used it on virtually every shot of the cornfield and then added laser blasts, dust, and special lighting effects to create the final amazing sequence. The teamwork needed to create a sequence such as this one explains a lot about the thrill of creative and visual problem-solving in the special effects department.

Dynamic visual effects such as surging sewer water in *Ratatouille* (OPPOSITE, BELOW) and laser beams in *Chicken Little* (ABOVE) add excitement to action packed sequences.

Light Me Up

Up until now, our CG sets and props have been viewed under simple work lights. Not unlike the rehearsals for a stage play, the lighting crew turns on the work lights in our digital set so that the actors and director can see what they are doing as the show is being roughed out. Now that animation is complete and approved, it's time for the **LIGHTERS** to go to work on the final lighting. Much like the lighting designer would do in a theater, a lighter on a CG film shines lights on the set and characters to illuminate the action, and more important, to create a mood and color palette for the story.

Working closely with the art director and layout crew, lighting designers create a preliminary lighting plan for the show. This is crucial because lighting determines not only what the audience sees but also what the audience *feels* about what they are seeing. It's a job that often balances subtle emotions. For example, a dim set lit with cool light can suggest loneliness or even fright, but it can also seem romantic, depending on the dramatic needs of the scene. A set full of light can be joyful, but it can also seem hot and oppressive.

Once an overarching color plan is set, lighters start to set general lights for individual sequences in the film. Much as on a live-action movie set, the lighter will create an overall lighting scheme, and then focus in on each individual shot to make minor adjustments. They take several passes at any one scene, working on every aspect of the lighting.

Lighters have to understand the complexities of how light works on any surface and texture, and they use their software tools to move lights around the set, place patterns (called gobos) over the light, or focus light on a small but important part of the scene. It's just like good theatrical lighting, but with unlimited digital lights.

Once the main lights are working on an object, the lighter can render up a simple "color pass"

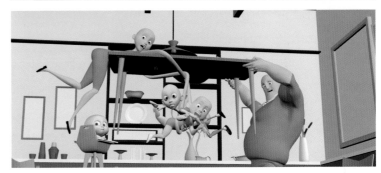

of the scene to get a feel for the lighting (often without highlights, reflections, or shadows at this point). Then, the lighter can turn individual lights on and off to work on each detailed component (the highlights, reflections, and shadows) or special effects element (smoke, water, dust, particles, atmosphere) to make sure the lights work well on those more ethereal objects. Working on lighting one element at a time allows changes to be made quickly and surgically, without taking valuable computer time and memory to re-render the entire scene every time something is changed.

This stage is a good time to re-examine the scene's cinematography. Does the virtual lens—close-up, wide-angle, telephoto—look correct? Are the characters composed in an interesting way on the screen? When a character moves fast, motion-blur tools can simulate the blur that happens in live films. It all helps transport the audience into the plausible alternate reality that the filmmakers have created for the movie.

The road from story sketch to final color begins with modelers who build the characters and sets in the computer. The layout crew places the characters in the set and locates the camera to best tell the story. Animators create a performance with low-resolution versions of the characters that are then shaded with textures, lit with digital lights and composited together into the final frame of the film as portrayed in these series of images from *The Incredibles* (OPPOSITE) and *Ratatouille* (ABOVE AND BELOW); TOP LEFT: Story sketch of Linguini and Colette by Ted Mathot.

Compositing and Rendering

ABOVE: The *Cars* gang gets modeled and then are animated in fairly low resolution. Later, the characters are more fully rendered and lit. Ray-tracing software (OPPOSITE, CENTER AND BELOW) tracks the lighting around the cars to account for reflections in paint and chrome; OPPOSITE, TOP: Computer graphics on film had its roots in the 1982 film *TRON*.

A computer can only hold so much data before it starts getting really slow and cranky. So up until now, all the elements of a scene have been tested individually, and at a low resolution in order to conserve computer space. But at the compositing and rendering stage, it's finally showtime! Time to turn up all the resolution and turn on all the lights, textures, effects, bells, and whistles to assemble the final shot that will appear on opening night.

This can create a huge, mind-numbing amount of work for the computer. Imagine rendering a scene for *Cars* with dozens of race cars on the track and thousands of fans cheering in the background. The computer actually calculates the direction and intensity of all the reflected lights on the chrome and paint for each highly reflective car (a process called ray tracing) so that the shot has a brilliant, realistic sense of lighting. It's not unusual for a single frame of a scene like this to take dozens of hours to com-

pute and render. There are twenty-four frames like this for every second of film, so even if the shot is just one second long, it could take many, many days to render.

This is all a bit scary. A huge room full of computers called a "render farm" is needed to composite all the elements of just one animated scene. The amazingly patient and diligent people who babysit the render farm have to keep an eye on the data 24/7. They monitor all the computers in the farm, troubleshoot stuck material, and diagnose any problems before they escalate.

The amount of data generated by the rendering of a single shot is so massive that, as soon as the shot is viewed and approved (usually with a huge sigh of relief), the data is taken off the system and stored to make room for other shots. If the scene has a mistake in it, it has to go back through the system for repairs and wait in the rendering queue again for another take at the final render. If everything works, the shot goes to the film editor to be cut into the story reel.

The final color shots get completed one shot at a time, and not in any specific order. An easy close-up shot of a single character in the middle of the movie might be completed in color early in production. The complex shot right next to it—a shot with loads of characters and effects that needed special tools developed for its completion—might not be finished until two years later. The movie comes together bit by bit, like a mosaic, until the whole movie is in color.

Performance Capture

ABOVE: An actress provides live-action reference for *Cinderella*.

Performance capture (also called motion capture or mocap) is a way of creating animation by digitally capturing a human performance. Typically, the human actor or dancer wears a tight-fitting suit covered with reference points that look like small dots. While the actor moves, cameras placed to capture all angles record that movement into a computer, which sees those dots as points in space and records their location as data. This motion-capture performance can then be used to drive the animation of a CG character.

The camera movements in the mocap process are often manipulated by a camera operator, who uses controls similar to the wheels that control a live-action movie camera, navigating the virtual camera through virtual space. This gives the camera movements a very natural, human quality.

Human reference is nothing new to animation, going back to the films *Snow White and the Seven Dwarfs*, *Cinderella*, and *Peter Pan*, to name a few, for which extensive live action was shot as reference for the character animators. This was particularly worthy as a tool for human characters, because audiences can be really intolerant of human animation if it doesn't seem right.

In the digital era, mocap takes performances directly from humans and translates them into digital data that can then be modified, enhanced, or combined with multiple takes to create a single, unified performance. The technique was pioneered by, among others, Weta Digital in New Zealand, for the Gollum character in The Lord of the Rings, and it was used again by Peter Jackson on the character King Kong. Some of the dance animation in *Happy Feet* used mocap, as did director Bob Zemeckis for his films *Polar Express*, *Beowulf*, and *A Christmas Carol*.

One of the most interesting applications of mocap is in *Pirates of the Caribbean: Dead Man's Chest*, wherein actor Bill Nighy and his "shipmates" each performed wearing a mocap suit covered with reference dots and stripes. Visual effects artists took the data from those raw performances and refined the animation, adding digital costumes and makeup elements to develop the amazing on-screen characters of Davy Jones and the crew of the *Flying Dutchman*. Most people are surprised when they learn that Davy Jones is a completely digital character.

Mocap is gaining popularity for animation production, but, as with any new technique, it has detractors. Some think it is not really animation at all; others see the performances as being stiff and mannequinlike. Of course, many see it as no different from the technique of using live action to drive human animation that Walt Disney developed for *Snow White and the Seven Dwarfs*. The mocap technique, still in its infancy, will be a permanent part of any animation filmmaker's toolbox.

Davy Jones and the crew of the *Flying Dutchman* from *Pirates of the Caribbean*: *Dead Man's Chest* are completely computer generated. Actors in motion-capture suits (ABOVE) are filmed on set, then modeled, lit (RIGHT), and combined with a live-action background to create the final scene (BELOW).

THE ALCHEMY OF ANIMATION

"All you can do sometimes is just press harder on your pencil to try to make the drawing express what you're feeling in your heart, and you hope that the audience can feel it as they're looking at it." — *Glen Keane*

Final frame from *Bambi*.

2-D Hand-Drawn Production

The technique of hand-drawn animation spans more than one hundred years and includes everything from Mickey Mouse cartoons to *Snow White and the Seven Dwarfs* to *The Lion King*. It's very much alive today in the films *Enchanted* and the upcoming *The Princess and the Frog*, among others. You'll notice that many of the terms discussed in 3-D production show up here. That's because the approach to staging and acting that we see in 3-D animation has its roots in 2-D animation.

Pre-production for 2-D starts very much like it would on any animated film: a script is written, storyboards are drawn and redrawn, and the world of the film is explored and designed. The narrative is broken down into sequences for production: the escape sequence, the love sequence, the fight sequence, the happy-ending sequence . . . you get the idea. Each sequence contains several individual scenes or shots. Each time you cut to a new angle, it's called a scene. A typical movie might have twenty-five sequences and about thirteen hundred individual scenes.

Design and Planning

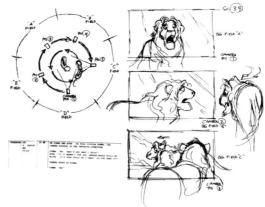

Once the foundation for the film is laid, the **LAYOUT ARTIST** begins working with the director and the art director to design the sets for the film. The set may be a small bedroom or a huge castle, but each location must tell the audience something about the character's personality and the story. When rough set drawings are finished, the layout artist takes the storyboards and begins working on a series of thumbnail drawings that will illustrate how every scene in a sequence will look. These drawings determine the camera angle, how the camera moves, the lighting values, and the path of action for the character. The result is a kind of technical version of the storyboard called a "workbook."

Once the workbook is complete, the individual shots are discussed and debated with other department heads to make sure the scene accommodates the needs of animators, background painters, and visual effects artists. After the director's approval, the layout artist draws a large version of each individual scene on animation paper.

At this point, the layout drawing looks just like an empty stage set waiting for the actors to enter. As this is a hand-drawn medium, the literal size of the drawing is chosen to make it a convenient and easy size for the animators to draw, depending on the complexity of the scene. A simple single-character shot with no camera move will be set up on standard "16 field" paper (paper that is sixteen inches wide). If the shot calls for a character to move side to side, the

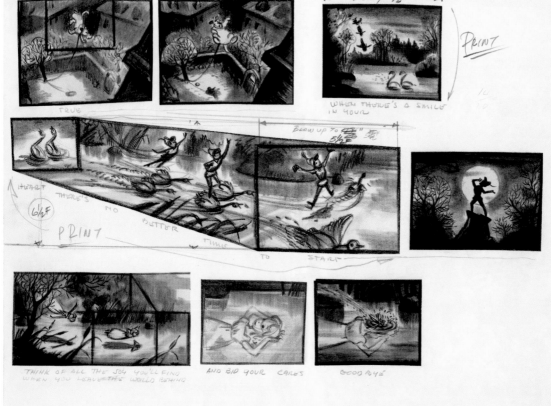

PREVIOUS PAGES: Publicity image from *The Princess and the Frog* and final frame from *The Lion King* (INSET); TOP: Art director Andy Gaskill's plan for a complex camera move for *The Lion King*; LEFT: Ken O'Connor's workbook sketches from *Peter Pan* indicate the camera placement and movement for each shot.

layout might be two or three fields (thirty-two or forty-eight inches) wide. A shot with hundreds of characters and multiple levels of background art will probably be set up on "24 field" paper or larger (twenty-four inches wide and extra tall, to make it easy for the animators to draw the "hundreds of characters").

On a separate piece of paper, the layout artist draws rough poses of the character to show the animator the size of the character and the path of action for the scene. Special effects, props, and other elements are also drawn into the layout, so the animators have a complete road map of how the scene will work. In a modern studio, the artists may use a digital tablet and stylus instead of paper and pencil to set up these layout elements, but the idea is the same regardless of the tools.

ABOVE: Each shot in the film is carefully planned and drawn. These layouts from *Lady and the Tramp* will become the set where the actor will perform.

In 2-D animation, the layout artist creates the illusion of depth on the screen using only a flat two-dimensional drawing. To accomplish this, many layouts are broken into simple planes—foreground, middle ground, distant ground. Moving the camera through these planes creates the illusion of dimension. As the camera moves through the scene, each plane or level of the scene can be calculated to move at a different speed, creating the illusion of depth and space.

Early experiments using individual planes of art to create the illusion of depth led to the invention of the multiplane camera in the 1930s. During a multiplane shot, each level (or plane) of the scene is painted on a piece of glass. Each level of glass is then suspended under the animation camera at a carefully calculated distance. As the camera moves down through each plane of glass, it creates a depth of field that looks amazingly real. (Don't worry—the camera doesn't break the glass. The camera moves down until it can't move any farther; then, that plane of glass is physically removed so the camera can begin moving down toward the next plane.) This labor-intensive process was replaced in the 1990s by a digital version. Unlike historic multiplane shots, a CG multiplane can contain dozens of levels of material and the camera moves can be infinite.

FAR LEFT: Ken Anderson's detailed design drawings of the interior of Roger and Anita's flat in London for *One Hundred and One Dalmatians*; LEFT: An early Disney innovation, the multiplane camera, created depth by filming through multiple layers of artwork painted on glass.

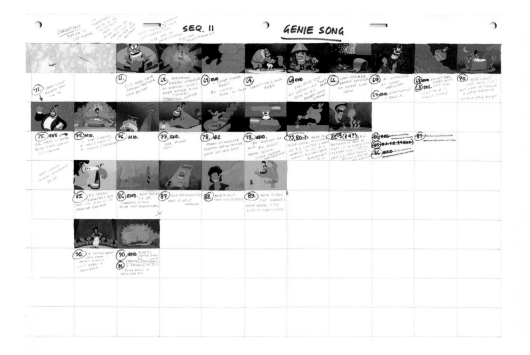

ABOVE: An art director's color script for the Genie's song in *Aladdin*; BELOW: Mike Giamo's color exploration for *Pocahontas*; OPPOSITE: The backgrounds for *Lilo & Stitch* were painted in watercolors, a very difficult, but beautiful, technique.

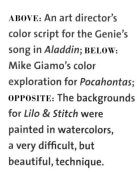

The job of a **BACKGROUND PAINTER** may seem obvious at first—create a painting based exactly on the predetermined layout, only full of color, light, and mood that serves as a backdrop for the characters on-screen. But additionally, the background artist collaborates closely with the **ART DIRECTOR** to plot the flow of color through a movie. This color-flow planning is particularly crucial in a 2-D film, because the color is created by paintings, not by lighting within a virtual environment. If it's done right, the viewer will have a physical reaction to color that will enhance the emotional impact of the story in a big way.

The balance of color, light, and shadow on the screen has to perfectly complement the animation, keeping the audience focused on the character and the story. Many factors are at play: where is the character in the background? What time of day is it? At what point does this scene appear in the movie? Is the moment sad or mysterious or celebratory?

"Whenever we're considering what to do with a shot," says *Chicken Little*'s art director Ian Gooding, "the first question we have to answer is 'what's the shot about?' It's our job to make sure the subject of the shot is the first thing that catches the audience's attention. Everything else

5000

LiLO   SEQ. 12.7   SC. 68.5

in the frame plays second fiddle to that."

During the planning process, painters will execute several small color sketches of various key moments in the film. These sketches provide a color map for the film, ensuring that the overall movie isn't too dark or light, and that it doesn't stray toward one color or another.

After this planning process is complete, the most important establishing backgrounds, called "color keys," are painted to set the color palette and style for each sequence of action. Then, the background artists begin the demanding process

of creating hundreds of individual paintings to provide the background for each and every scene. Many of the early Disney films were painted with watercolor, gouache, or oil paints, but now most backgrounds are painted digitally with programs including Photoshop, Painter, or Illustrator.

Remember that the background is just that—a background. It's a stage to support the characters, not to detract from them. The most important aspect of the final background painting is that it contributes to the emotional content of the scene.

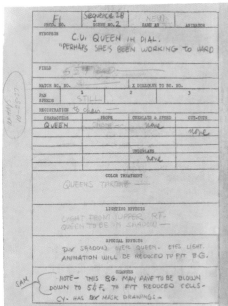

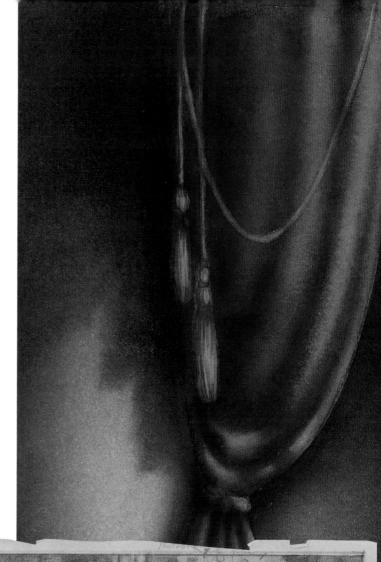

THESE PAGES: This exquisite background from *Snow White and the Seven Dwarfs* began as sketches in pencil and gouache (TOP). The final layout, a pencil drawing, sits atop the final production background. The flap of paper taped to the layout gives information on artists and camera movements.

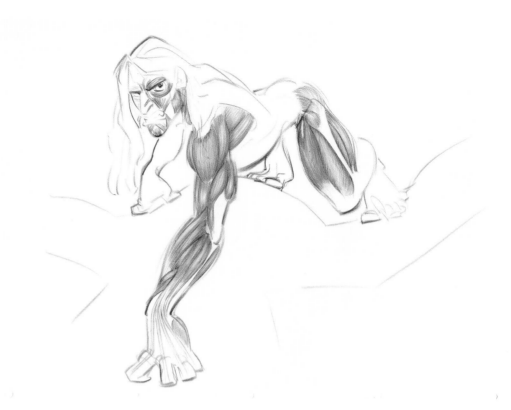

RIGHT: Glen Keane drew this study of Tarzan's underlying muscle structure. Studies like this and the thumbnails from *One Hundred and One Dalmatians* (BELOW) help the actor prepare for the performance; OPPOSITE: The Beast uses his whole body to express anger and resignation.

An Actor with a Pencil

Imagine you're a famous actor who has just been hired to appear in a big-budget movie. You read the script, study your lines, and do wardrobe and hair tests. On your first day of shooting, you arrive on the movie set, but just as the cameras are about to roll, the director says, "Here's a pencil, I want you to draw your performance instead." That's what a 2-D animator does every day.

As with any actor, preparation is everything. Photos, books, movies, and other references help inspire the performance, with help from an animator's biggest tool: observation. Each animator's preparation is very personal and often intense. On *Beauty and the Beast*, animator Glen Keane covered the walls of his room with drawings of wild animals such as lions, wolves, bears, and bison. He spent days drawing nothing but horns. He went to the London Zoo and got as close to the gorillas as the animal handler would allow in order to get the feeling for the weight and size of Beast. This preparation is a way for the animators to subconsciously immerse themselves in the character.

The animation principles discussed in 3-D are still the same in 2-D (in fact they came from 2-D). They are:

Think, Plan, Animate, "Plus" it.

But there is another hidden secret behind the art of great animation:

EMOTION.

Great animators put themselves into a character's shoes in order to empathize with it and find the best way to channel that character's emotions through their pencil and onto the paper.

Every nuance in a drawing matters. The expression on a character's face is a window into its thoughts and desires. The eyes in particular are the first place the audience might look to get a clue to the feelings and emotions of a character in a scene. The body's posture and "attitude" telegraph emotions as well. Then, the timing of the animation breathes life into the character. Once again, movement and rest are equally important in creating a living, thinking character. This holds true for both comedy and drama. Part of the amazing appeal of hand-drawn animation is that it is done by hand, through a pencil, and projected onto the screen, where it is transmitted directly into the eyes and hearts of the audience. It is a very personal expression of an idea.

Characters and their emotions make stories come to life. So determining the character's emotional background is the first priority of the animator before any actual animation takes place.

TOP: In this rough animation, Pinocchio has no eyes and very simple features, but his action is clear and simple. Details can be added later; ABOVE: Glen Keane's very powerful rough animation from *The Fox and the Hound*.

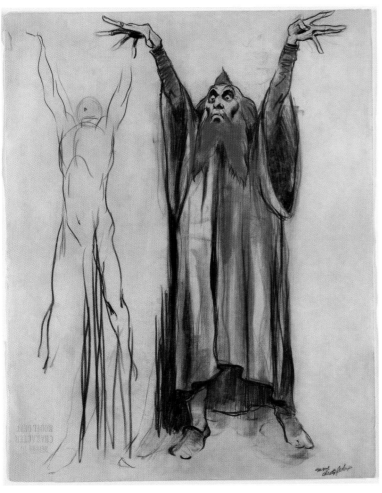

- ➤ **What is the character's personal history before the start of the film?**
- ➤ **What are the stakes of this story?**
- ➤ **What is at risk for any given character and why should the audience root for him/ her?**
- ➤ **What does the character want and why can't he have it?**
- ➤ **How does she feel about herself?**
- ➤ **Does he like himself? Do we like him?**
- ➤ **What are his fears and weaknesses?**
- ➤ **What's her environment: cluttered, clean, country, city, rich, poor, hostile, friendly?**
- ➤ **What changes his life during the movie?**
- ➤ **Where is she headed after the movie?**

Understanding what is under the skin of the character, both literally, as in this life drawing of the Sorcerer (LEFT), and emotionally, like in these powerful iconic Bill Tytla drawings (BELOW) of Chernabog from *Fantasia*'s "Night on Bald Mountain."

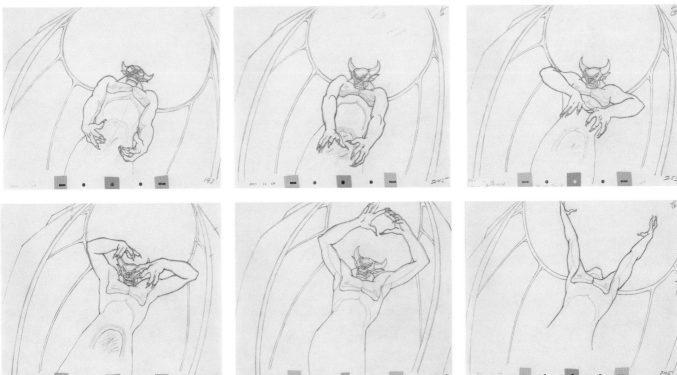

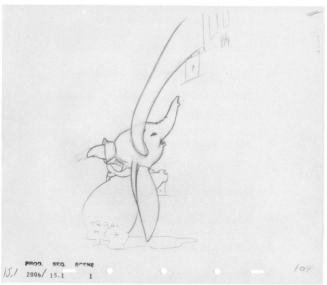

Another way to drive the emotion in animation is to work with the forces that affect the characters. Acting is in large part *re-acting* to forces that confront the character. Sometimes, those forces are physical, such as a slap in the face or a raging windstorm. But other forces are emotional—betrayal, love, greed, loss, distrust, joy, doubt. Forces help inform the performance of every character on the screen.

Think, plan, animate, and "plus it" all with heart and real emotion. Master animators Frank Thomas and Ollie Johnston summarize the essence of an animator's job this way:

THINK *first, draw last. Have a clear and positive idea in your head before you start. If you go into a piece of acting with a vague or ambiguous idea of what you will do, the work will be vague and ambiguous. Make bold choices. The animator will flounder with indecision unless he can get inside the character and know precisely what actions are right for that personality. As long as there is any confusion, the drawings will be vague and indecisive.*

THIS PAGE: These *Dumbo* drawings have a wonderful appeal and translate a range of emotions; OPPOSITE: Clean-up animation of a Bob Carlson scene from the short *Jack and Old Mac.*

10

Clean-up

The animator draws a stack of drawings that, when filmed and viewed at twenty-four frames per second, create the illusion of life. This filmed "pencil test" of the animator's rough drawings was an innovation in the early days of the Walt Disney Studio, when personality animation was in its infancy. In a modern studio, the animator's pencil drawings are scanned into a computer that plays the drawings back on a monitor. The animator can sync the drawings to the sound track, make changes to the scene's timing, then critique the animation with the director before making the corrections and "plusses" that every scene needs. When the scene works perfectly in this rough stage, the drawings move on to be cleaned up for the final line drawings that will appear on the screen.

Just as everyone's handwriting is slightly different, every animator has his or her own personal style. So the supervising animator (a lead animator on a character) draws a series of "model sheets" to show all the animators on a film how to draw the character. Still, given the variety of individual styles, some drawings will be "on model," while some will be a little "off model." Some animators draw very loose, expressive drawings, while others draw more precisely. It's the job of the **CLEAN-UP ARTIST** to make sure every drawing is "on model."

The character Tarzan, for instance, was supervised by Glen Keane, but drawn by as many as eight different animators on his crew at studios in Paris and Burbank. Each artist had a slightly different individual style. The clean-up artist pulls all these diverse personal styles together.

The clean-up artist starts with the animator's extreme drawings. A fresh piece of paper is put over the animator's rough drawing and the artist makes a new, beautifully cleaned-up drawing. Clean-up artists collaborate closely with the animators to make sure the nuance of the animation doesn't get lost when the scene gets redrawn.

Then, the action between these cleaned-up extreme drawings (or "keys") is further broken down with drawings called "breakdowns." Finally, the action is broken down even further, so that there is a single, unique drawing for every frame of film. The final drawings that fill in all the frames of action are called "inbetweens."

Studios are now experimenting with digital drawing tablets as a tool for clean-up artists. The work is similar, but instead of cleaning up drawings on paper, the clean-up artist draws directly onto a digital monitor. New tools allow them to quickly flip back and forth between dozens of drawings and should even help 2-D clean-up artists with some of the more repetitive parts of their job. But, as with all tools, it's the artist that drives the animation—the computer only helps.

OPPOSITE: Clean-up drawings must still define anatomy, form, mass, volume, and detail without sacrificing the animation or acting. This cleaned-up Shere Khan has it all; as does Captain Hook (ABOVE); LEFT AND BELOW: Tarzan as an animator's "rough" and in the corresponding clean-up.

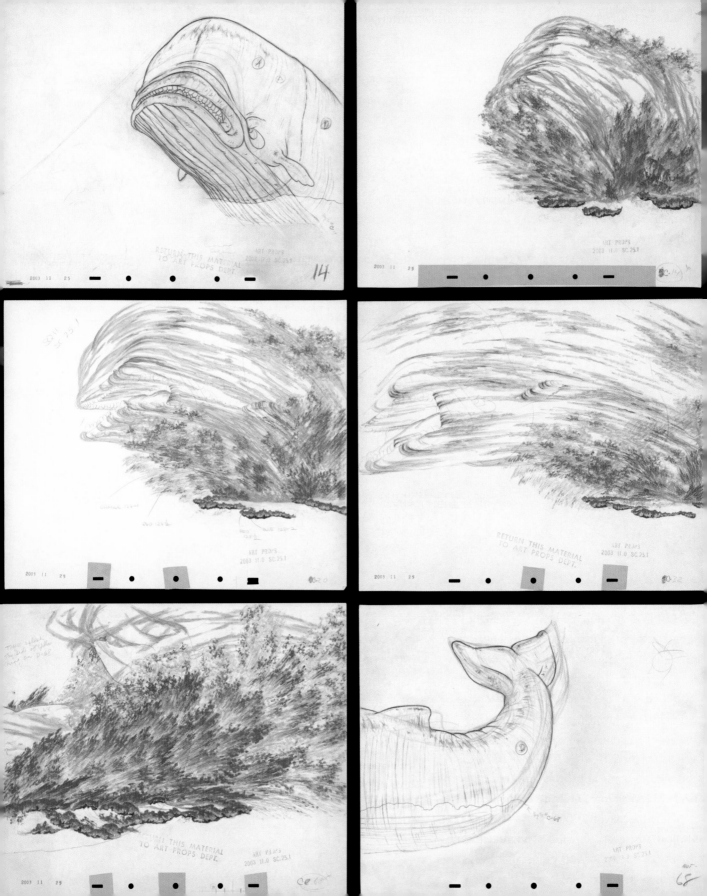

Water, Wind, and Flame

When the character animators and clean-up artists are finished with their work, the effects animator inherits the scene, adding shadows, props, and forces of nature. The effects animator adds literally everything that moves on the movie screen, other than the character itself. The technique is the same as that in character animation: draw the extremes of the action first and then follow up with additional drawings (breakdowns and inbetweens) to break the animation into twenty-four frames a second.

Traditional effects animators now have an arsenal of computer-based tools to create their work. For example, "particle" software can help the animator create and move flocks of particles around a screen. Then, the animator can assign an attribute—a snowflake, for example—to each particle. The result will appear like a flock of snowflakes flying around. The same tool can be used to create embers from a fire or particles of dust in a light shaft. Other CG tools help the 2-D animator with complex crowd scenes or vehicle animation.

The 2-D effects animator also can draw on traditional tools—including pencils, pastels, or charcoal—to achieve a more hand-done look for a particular effect. The result can be a beautifully designed and rendered effect. Note the gigantic waves of water kicked up by Monstro the whale in *Pinocchio*.

In a 2-D film, effects are carefully designed to match the graphic style of the rest of the movie. Remember how the style of *Aladdin* was based on the unlikely combination of Persian art mixed with the simple cartoon style of caricaturist Al Hirshfeld? The effects animators studied Middle Eastern shapes, letters from alphabets, architecture, textiles, and fine art, using those typical shapes to inform the design of the visual effects for the film.

Study a sequence from *Lilo & Stitch* and you'll see a special effects animator's work in nearly every scene. Waves, water, shadows, surfboards, spaceships, semitrailers, laser canons, fire from tiki torches . . . the list goes on. Every effect demands a different approach and uses a different tool. It's this variety of visual problems and their ultimate solutions that make the special effects animator's job one of the most interesting on any movie.

Monstro (**OPPOSITE**) and Maleficent (**BELOW**) are both masterpieces of 2-D, hand-drawn effects animation.

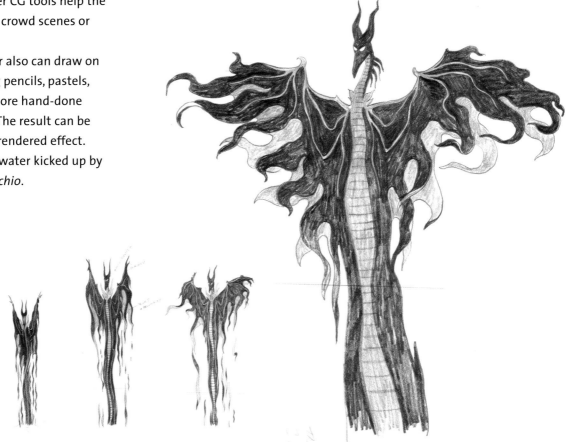

Ink and Paint

All the artwork in a given shot eventually arrives in the ink and paint department. Some of the material may be drawings on paper, and other material may be digitally created art. Any paper drawings are scanned into the computer at this point, so that all the elements of the scene exist in a digital format. A **COLOR MODELER** loads all the elements of a shot onto his or her computer screen. The digital artwork elements are stacked in layers in much the same way as the layers in a Photoshop file. The bottom layer is the painted color background. All the levels of character and effects art, as well as any overlays (foreground furniture, trees, etc.), are stacked on top of the background layer. The color modeler begins to select colors for characters, props, and effects, working closely with the art director and always referring back to the color script that the art director prepared in pre-production.

General color palettes are set for the characters in each sequence. Then, as work begins on the individual shots, the art director and color modeler can make slight changes to the color. Director-approved work travels on to the **PAINTERS**.

In animation's early days, the painters would work on clear plastic sheets called "cels" (short for celluloid). The animator's drawings would be traced onto the cel with ink, and then the cel would be turned over and painted on the reverse side with all the appropriate character

ABOVE: Inkers and painters chat with Walt Disney; RIGHT: Each color area on this drawing from *Three Little Pigs* is marked, numbered, and matched to a specific paint color in preparation for cel painting.

THE ALCHEMY OF ANIMATION

colors; hence the term "ink and paint." In most contemporary studios, the cleaned-up drawings are painted on a digital tablet that floods selected areas of the character with color. This painting software automates the process a bit so that the painter doesn't have to paint each individual drawing. It's still a time-consuming art, but it is all a part of bringing characters to life.

Painted characters are digitally composited over the background painting with special effects elements, CG elements, or other layout pieces, such as moving clouds or foreground

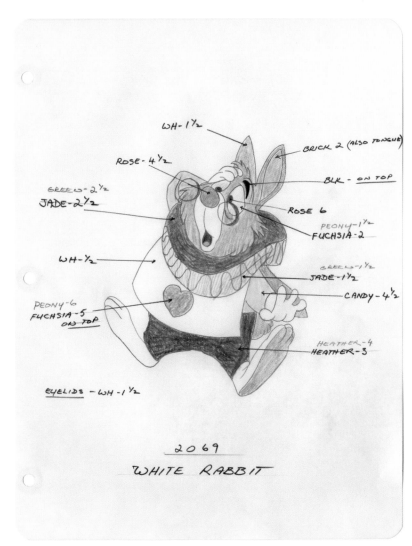

trees. Then, the composited frame is sent to the render farm to be rendered at the highest resolution needed for the final film.

After the fully composited and rendered version of the scene is cut into the story reel, the crew views the final color shot in "dailies" (a film term meaning "that day's work"). Because the needs and schedule of each individual shot are so complex, final color shots rarely are completed in continuity. If you were to look at the work reel during production on a 2-D film, you'd see story sketches cut together with pencil tests, clean-up tests, and final-color shots in a haphazard montage. It's only a few months before the release date that all the color gets cut into the reel. Along the way, if there is a problem with the scene, it will go back to be fixed and re-composited. When all the color work is complete, the final data is taken off the system and archived along with all drawings for the scene.

Color-model mark-up drawings give the painters instructions on each color area of a character. Compare the mark-ups for *Alice in Wonderland* (ABOVE) and *The Lion King* (LEFT) and you'll see that the process hasn't changed much even now in the digital era.

"There is an energy with stop-motion that you can't even describe. It's got to do with giving things life, and I guess that's why I wanted to get into animation originally."—*Tim Burton*

Stop-Motion Production

Stop-motion animation is one of the oldest forms of animation. The earliest stop-motion animators used a motion-picture camera that could shoot a puppet or an object one frame at a time, making small animation adjustments for each frame. When played back at twenty-four frames per second, the puppet would appear to come to life. The original 1933 version of *King Kong* and Ray Harryhausen's early *Jason and the Argonauts* (1963) and later *Clash of the Titans* (1981) are some of the best examples of stop-motion animation.

The story and design aspects of a stop-motion movie are nearly identical to the development of a 2-D or 3-D film, but when it comes to production, the approach to getting the film onto the screen is much more similar to that of a live-action movie.

PREVIOUS PAGES: Final frames of Jack Skellington from *The Nightmare Before Christmas*; OPPOSITE: Tim Burton sketch for *The Nightmare Before Christmas*; ABOVE: *Noah's Ark*, a simple stop-motion film made at Disney, was nominated for an Academy Award for best animated short in 1959.

Set Design

After a pre-production period of design and story development, the first production step on a stop-motion film is set construction. Unlike a live-action film, where the sets are typically flimsy and temporary, a stop-motion film's sets must be really solid—they'll have to take a lot of abuse from the animators and camera department.

All the set details and supporting structures must be robust enough to withstand the stress of long days and the rigors of real lights and cameras. If the set jiggles, melts, or falls apart during shooting, then you've just lost dozens of hours of an animator's work.

The sets must have access for the animators to work with their characters, so hidden trap doors and breakaway sections of set pieces are the norm. Although sets are scaled down to tabletop proportions, they vary in detail and size depending upon how much the set is featured in the film. Spaces closest to the characters will get the most attention, and distant buildings or landscapes get a simpler treatment. The finished sets are decorated with appropriately scaled versions of furniture, carpets, window dressing, and props. Very little of this set dressing can be purchased, so most is custom-built for the scale and physical demands of each set. The final dressed set is then weathered and aged to give the space a lived-in look.

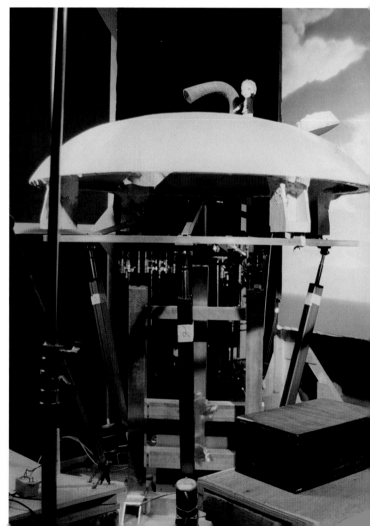

OPPOSITE, TOP: Set design starts with a simple sketch like this one from *Frankenweenie*.
OPPOSITE AND ABOVE: Sets for *Tim Burton's The Nightmare Before Christmas* and *James and the Giant Peach* are built off the ground and must pull apart for easy access by animators, lighting, and cameras.

Puppets

As with any animation technique, the top priority for a stop-motion character animator is bringing the characters to life. In stop-motion, the characters actually exist as tangible, three-dimensional puppets.

Life for a character puppet starts with a traditional process of designs and drawings based on the story. Sculptors then create a clay version of the character, which, as with the other types of animation, is called a maquette. In 2-D and 3-D animation, the maquette is mostly for exploration and reference, but in stop-motion, the sculpture is literally used as the final representation of the character in every detail. It will also be the basis for the important underlying skeleton within the character called an "armature." Armatures are made of steel or aluminum, along with wire or whatever other material may be needed to support the puppet. The **ARMATURE MAKERS** start by researching

how the character needs to move. They need to allow for joints and pivot points that will give complete flexibility to the puppet, yet still allow the puppet be easily controlled by the animator.

The armature also has to hold its position without moving or falling over. It's not as simple as it sounds, especially if the character is top heavy, as with Oogie Boogie from *Tim Burton's The Nightmare Before Christmas*. If a character's eyes are built into the armature, the armature maker has to consider how the eyes and lids will move. The screws or control points to move the eyes have to be hidden in the hair, in the ears, or under the clothes of a character. Multiple armatures are built for each character so there will be extra puppets should something go wrong during production, or if two animators need the same puppet at the same time.

After the details of the armature are settled, the character sculpture is cast and a mold is made, usually of plaster, though occasionally of fiberglass (again, for creating a series of identical puppets). Once the mold is created, the armature is placed inside the empty mold and the mold is sealed. Foam latex is injected into the mold, which completely surrounds the armature, creating an exact replica of the character with a movable steel skeleton inside.

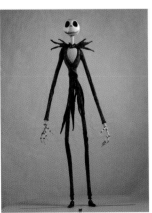

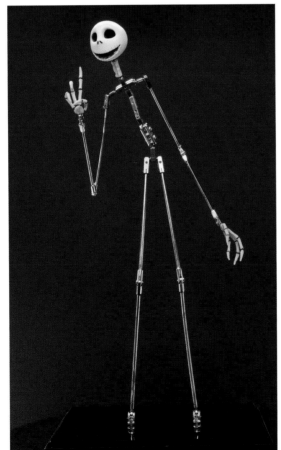

OPPOSITE: Character designs by Tim Burton; ABOVE: An armature rests underneath the foam and fabric exterior of a puppet. Jack's armature (RIGHT) was about twelve inches tall and had to be tiny to fit inside his thin legs and arms; TOP RIGHT: The final head for the Sally puppet.

Jack's heads (LEFT AND ABOVE) were all replaceable. Animators had to select the correct head for the attitude of dialogue and expression; OPPOSITE: The completed Oogie Boogie puppet.

Makeup and Wardrobe

The finished casting of the puppet goes to be dressed and groomed. First, the surface of the puppet is cleaned with alcohol to prepare it for painting. The long hours under camera lights and in the hands of animators require the paints and costumes to be very sturdy. Some clothes are painted on, whereas others require costumers to make the puppets' often elaborate wardrobes. Finally, eyelashes and hair are attached to the puppet one strand at a time. The hair is styled and the puppet is ready for action.

The faces on characters such as Jack Skellington are a little different from the bodies because they're not animated with movable armatures; instead, they have replaceable heads. Each head has a different expression, and the animator selects the heads for each frame based on the emotion, dialogue, and acting required for that moment. This means literally hundreds of individual heads need to be sculpted, cast, painted, and maintained for the animators to do their work.

Many of the props have to be rigged to move, too. Santa's "naughty or nice" list in *Tim Burton's The Nightmare Before Christmas* looks like it's written on paper, but the list was actually constructed with a sheet of aluminum foil sandwiched between two sheets of thin paper. This let the animator move the list in small increments so they could shoot one frame at a time without it flopping around uncontrollably.

ABOVE AND OPPOSITE, BELOW: Costume and makeup details are sewn with fabric and thread that are in scale to the puppets from *The Nightmare Before Christmas* and *James and the Giant Peach*; OPPOSITE, TOP: Oogie is painted and aged in a paint booth at the studio fabrication shop.

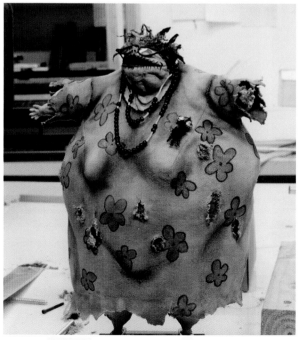

TOP AND ABOVE: A sea of teapot-shaped clouds is difficult to light and move; LEFT: An animator reaches up through the clouds to make an adjustment on the Jack puppet; OPPOSITE: The sets for *James and the Giant Peach* were very large with multiple layers of scrim to create the illusion of depth and atmosphere on this icy sea.

Lights, Camera . . .

Stop-motion and live action have a lot in common when it comes to lighting and cinematography. A cinematographer paints with light. The set and characters by themselves only have about half of the amount of mood and expression that the story demands. The cinematographer—with the help of an electrician called a **GAFFER**—begins by placing lights around the set in preparation for shooting. These lights form an ambient lighting design for each scene, but as the camera moves in for a close-up or changes to another angle, the lights have to be adjusted to make the new angle work. As in live action, the lights can be covered with colored gel or cropped with "barn doors," "snouts," "gobos," and "flags"—all of which are tools to focus the light on a part of the set.

If the story demands atmosphere like fog or rain, the crew has to plan which effects can be handled practically on the set and which need to be added by effects animators in post production. The cinematographer also works with lenses and lens filters to create certain effects.

The Puppet Masters

Once all the puppets and sets are prepared, dressed, and lit, it's time for the animator to go to work. A stop-motion animator has to use a puppet to create a living being. In short, they are miracle workers. Each animator is in search of the perfect gesture or subtle acting idea that will tell the story and make the character live.

Animators start with a pose test, or "pop through," of the scene, where the character is held for ten or twenty frames and the path of action is established. After discussion with the director and the usual thinking and planning, the long process of capturing the scene one frame at a time begins.

The physical demands of shooting stop-motion animation are staggering. Imagine a set with multiple characters. An animator has to crawl into the set from a trap door or a side angle and then move all the characters a small amount with finesse and grace, keeping track of each movement individually. Then, the animator has to sneak out of the frame without disturbing anything. One frame of film is exposed. Then, the animator crawls back in, adjusts all the characters, and shoots a single frame again... and again... and again. Once the animators start, they will want to finish a shot as quickly as they can before anything goes wrong. It's not unusual to go through several twelve- to fourteen-hour days of physical labor to film just a few precious seconds of animation. It's also not unusual to have systems in place on the set to check for burned-out light bulbs or unexpected fluctuations in voltage that might dim the lights and ruin a scene.

A motion-control computer manages the camera movement, so the motion is solid and even. But some times it may be more practical for the camera to be moved manually, frame by frame, to track the action. Modern stop-motion films are shot on digital, single-lens reflex cameras at high resolution. During the shot, digital frames are uploaded into a computer, allowing the animator to see the motion immediately, without waiting a day for the film to be processed and returned. Early stop-motion had no preview feature like this, and

RIGHT: A *Nightmare* animator spends hours in a small set while animating multiple characters; OPPOSITE PAGE: Animators adjust the character's pose and movement before shooting each frame of film.

THE ALCHEMY OF ANIMATION

even recently animators had to rely on a small video-assist camera strapped to the side of the film camera lens in order to preview their action. Today, the animator has the benefit of viewing the final frames on the computer screen while they are working.

"Plussing" a shot in stop-motion is difficult, if not impossible, once the animator has done the hard work of making the scene come to

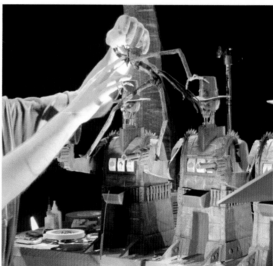

life. Unlike 2-D or 3-D animation, a stop-motion animator would have to scrap an entire scene and start over again if something needed to be corrected or improved.

The finished scenes head off into a post-production process that is essentially the same as the finishing process for 2-D and digital 3-D films.

THE ALCHEMY OF ANIMATION

Joe Grant's drawing of twin tigers for *The Lion King*.

Finishing Touches and Post Production

Years of planning and work lead to the moment of final assembly on a film. Putting all the diverse elements of sound and picture together on the screen is a very tough job that usually takes place under great deadline pressure. The film's release date is coming! This part of the process is called "post production."

There are a million details to manage during the final days of post production on an animated film. The **POST PRODUCTION SUPERVISOR** wrangles all these details while keeping the picture on schedule and budget. All the recording studios and mix facilities need to be booked ahead of time, technical specifications must be sent to the facilities, and quality has to be balanced with cost and the schedule. It is one of the most stressful jobs on a film. The post supervisor needs to balance the creative needs of the director with the harsh reality that time is running out and the release date is immovable. It's even more complex when there are international releases in multiple languages on multiple release platforms (film, digital cinema, DVD, TV) that now can include even "stereo 3-D" versions of the film that have to be finished with 3-D glasses, special projectors, and screens. Pixar's *Toy Story 3* will be in "stereo 3-D" along with most all of the upcoming animated releases from Disney and Pixar.

OPPOSITE: With the advent of digital projection, the stereo 3-D process creates a whole new experience for the audience.

Cutting and Trimming

The editor, who has nurtured the film every step of the way, still has important work to do during the post process, when most of the film crew is long gone. Editors have been on the movie from the start, building the earliest story reels and working through dozens of iterations of the film during production. Now the editor presides over final sweatbox sessions and starts to collaborate with music and sound editors to get all the sound and picture elements to the final sound-mixing stage, on schedule and with the highest quality.

It's worth pointing out that an editor's most important job on the film is "editing." When a crew spends years on a project, they sometimes lose perspective. At this final step of a film's production, a good editor can look at the film with a fresh eye and cut scenes or whole sequences that are too lengthy or that no longer fit the structure of the film. Using editorial computers that track picture, dialogue, music, and effects, an editor slowly chips away at anything extraneous or unclear until the film is as lean and entertaining as possible.

Music

Music has always been the centerpiece of Disney's animated films. Songs can tell a story in a very concentrated, emotional way. The musical "score" is the last layer of storytelling applied to a film, providing a beautiful harmony to the art on the screen.

The score **COMPOSER** has to be very focused on the story and the emotional content of the film. Up until now, all the artists have worked hard to tell the story with their performance or artistry. If their work does not evoke the desired emotion, the composer won't be able to help it much, but if everything is working well, then music can take the project to a whole new level.

The search for music starts early, when the director and producer listen to styles of music that might fit their story. Pre-existing movie sound tracks are the principle source of influence for a film's musical style, but classical and contemporary music can also provide a clue to the right musical feel. *Finding Nemo* director Andrew Stanton always wanted to work without literal songs, but with a score that could capture the ethereal universe under the sea. He not only listened to other sound tracks, but also cut representative pieces of music into the story reels to see how it felt with the story, including some by composer Thomas Newman. Newman, the composer for *The Shawshank Redemption* and *Pay It Forward*, turned out to be the perfect fit for *Finding Nemo*.

A composer may be chosen earlier, during pre-production—particularly if he or she has to write original songs for the film. But the largest share of the composer's work begins late in the

process. Composers start by watching the film with the director and talking about its central, overarching emotional themes. Then, a more detailed meeting called a "spotting session" takes place to plot out the approach to the score with the director. During this spotting session, a **MUSIC EDITOR** takes notes of each musical moment to begin breaking down the music into smaller bits called "cues."

Usually, a composer starts by writing the big themes for the characters and key moments in a film. If it's a musical, the melodies usually grow from the orchestral score. Then, the composer fits the themes more specifically into the scenes in the film, adjusting the tempo to sync with the rhythm of the characters.

ABOVE: Composer Danny Elfman during a scoring session for *Meet the Robinsons*; OPPOSITE: Bonnie Raitt and Alan Menken (TOP LEFT AND MIDDLE) at work on the music for *Home on the Range*; Randy Newman (TOP RIGHT) listens to playback with John Lasseter; James Newton Howard (BOTTOM LEFT) gives notes during an *Atlantis* scoring session; The band Barenaked Ladies (BOTTOM RIGHT) record their song for the *Chicken Little* sound track.

See Model
Flesh
Hair
Eyes
Eyebrows
mustache
Inside Lines on Suits
White 0
Outline Heavy
Inside Lines Normal
All Strings + Bows - Line 3 (NC)
on All Instruments
Stem - & Rests } Black
Balance - Purple 8 (NC)
1ST FOR THE LEFT SIDE
Chair - Black
this is not the final
H-

The goal of a good score is paradoxical, because you want to use every musical advantage to support the emotion of the film, but you don't want the audience to consciously notice the score. Elements of the score can really help transport the audience to another world. For example, Alan Silvestri traveled to Hawaii to record native Hawaiian singers for the sound track of *Lilo & Stitch*. Alan Menken went to a cathedral in Europe to record the church choirs and pipe organs that give *The Hunchback of Notre Dame* its celestial sound. Hans Zimmer used African instruments and choruses recorded in South Africa to evoke the rhythms of the Pride Lands in *The Lion King*.

ORCHESTRATORS assist the composer as part of the music team. They can help the composer deal with the huge volume of writing for a film by "voicing" the music to the various instruments in the orchestra. Their palette of instruments includes traditional orchestral sounds, synthesized sounds, native instruments, and, of course, choral work.

The music team also includes **COPYISTS**, who write out all the parts for the performers, and a music **CONTRACTOR**, who hires and supervises the musicians for the recording session itself. When all the elements are ready, a full orchestra of musicians shows up to

OPPOSITE: Musicians from the short *Toot, Whistle, Plunk and Boom*; ABOVE: A Hawaiian children's chorus contributed to the sound track of *Lilo & Stitch*; RIGHT: John Debney conducts the *Chicken Little* orchestra.

record the score. A **MUSICAL DIRECTOR** joins the music team to rehearse and conduct the orchestra and chorus while watching the film on a video monitor, ensuring that the music and the movie stay in perfect sync.

The **MUSIC EDITOR**, who has been in on all of the music planning sessions, is the composer's link to all the technical aspects of the score, making sure that everything is recorded in sync with the movie and is eventually delivered to the final mixing stage to be laid into the film mix.

A **MUSIC MIXER** is responsible for setting the microphones and recording levels to capture the musical performance "on tape." Literal recording tape is seldom used; rather, the recording is usually done directly to hard drives that are then supplied to the final dubbing stage through an all-digital pipeline. After the orchestra leaves, the composer and mixer spend several sessions together remixing the music in preparation for the final film and the sound track album.

LEFT: Kathryn Beaumont, the voice of Alice, plays in Jimmy Macdonald's jug band. Macdonald ran a very inventive sound-effects department for years at Disney, and even did the voice of Mickey Mouse.

Sound Design

If you stop for a minute and listen to all the sounds going on around you right now, you'll notice that the world is a noisy place. Sounds exist across a complete spectrum—volumes and textures from loud to soft, from high pitched tweeters to the bass sub-woofer that you feel in your chest.

Unlike on a live-action film, where you might capture some of the ambient sounds on the set, all the sounds of an animated movie have to be created after shooting. Sounds come to our ears in layers. There are the distant sounds of traffic or birds, and then there are more present sounds, such as the computer in front of you or your microwave oven. There are even very specific synchronous sounds, such as footsteps, and more punctuated sounds, such as an explosion or a slamming door. **SOUND EFFECTS EDITORS** create this audible world for the screen. And yes, like everyone else in the process, sound effects editors

tell the story, too. Just like the art director who plans for a full palette of colors for your eye, the sound team creates an effective palette of sounds for your ears. These sounds create a plausible reality for the characters in the film, and decisions made about sound will give the audience important clues about characters, emotions, and settings.

Sound designers create some custom sounds specifically for a film, such as the undulating sound of Beast's magic mirror, whereas other, more general sounds, such as dog barks or car horns, can be found in a sound-effects library. Sometimes, sounds are created in unlikely ways. Walking on Styrofoam peanuts sounds like walking in snow. Bending an old leather wallet can mimic the sound of a creaky wood floor.

Another way to make sounds is a process called "Foley," named after the man who invented it. In the Foley process, the movie is shown on a monitor while a **FOLEY ARTIST** performs sounds to match the picture. Footsteps, movement of cloth or paper, and any other sounds that have to synchronize closely with the picture are often recorded this way.

Sound design is a very iterative process. As the story reel and animation come together on a film, the sound editors will experiment with their sounds by test-running new sounds for the director at each screening. They keep the sounds that work and toss or redesign the ones that don't.

Mix It Up

It's time for the final mix: the process of taking hundreds of sounds that have been organized into three general groups—dialogue, music, and sound effects—and mixing them all together into a perfect sound track for the film. Most films are mixed with a five-speaker setup in mind: left, center, right, left surround, and right surround. If you have a home theater, you are already familiar with this. Filmmakers also use a seven-speaker configuration, which allows for four discreet channels of surround sound to bring the audience a fuller sound field with more detail and resolution.

The lead **RE-RECORDING MIXER** presides over a huge mixing panel with volume controls for each individual element of sound. The music editor and sound editor sit adjacent to the lead mixer on the mixing stage, making sure all the sound elements are supplied to the main mixing board in digital form. It's a very detailed job, because each footstep, inhalation, gust of wind, or twig snap is isolated on its own track so the mixers can manipulate the volume and shading of that particular sound in the mix. The director and mixers preview the movie for themselves several times to arrive at the right combination of dialogue, music, and sound effects that will best tell the story.

It's a delicate operation. The dialogue must be clear and understood, sound effects and Foley must reflect the environment, and music must fit into the mix in a way that that is emotionally supportive of the story, without distracting the audience.

Films now receive "day and date" releases in dozens of countries on the same date. For foreign-language versions, the mixers create a special sound track that includes only the music and sound effects. This "M & E" version of the film is then sent to local markets around the world in advance of the release so that each international market can cast actors and re-record the dialogue for the film in their own language. Each language track is combined with the M&E track, mixed, and married with the picture to create a complete version of the film in French, Italian, Mandarin, German, and just about any other language you can name.

ABOVE: Mixers adjust dialogue, music, and sound effects into perfect relationships for the final mix of the movie; BELOW: A typical configuration for a 7.1 sound set-up in your home.

Seven-speaker configuration

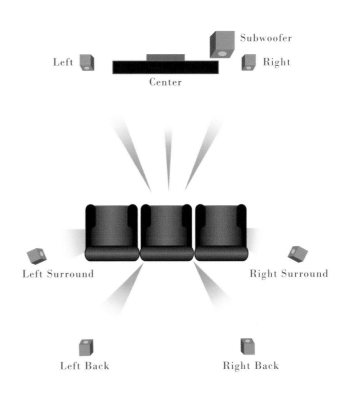

Left   Center   Subwoofer   Right

Left Surround   Right Surround

Left Back   Right Back

Digital Cinema

ABOVE AND INSET:
Digital-cinema theaters
project the movie from
a hard drive onto the
screen. The image is
made up of millions of
pixels, not unlike those
made by your color
TV—just much bigger
and more detailed;
OPPOSITE: Walt Disney
always believed in
marketing his characters
to his audiences (even
with Mickey Mouse
undies).

Just a few years ago, every movie theater projected 35mm film. The film was loaded onto giant, flat platters, and when the projectionist pressed the "start" button, the film looped down past the projector bulb and back onto the platter. Today, more and more theater owners have "gone digital." Instead of worrying about giant projectors and film that can scratch and break, digital cinemas can project an entire movie from a digital hard drive about the size of a ham sandwich.

The picture and sound track for a digital cinema presentation are exactly what the filmmakers intended. The color and nuance of every sound matches exactly what they heard when they were making the film.

So when it's opening night and there are no cans of film, it's not a problem with the advent of digital cinema. When color on a film is finished, hard drives that contain all the shots in the film go to a film lab where a **COLOR TIMER** will run through the material with the art director to make sure that the color in the movie is accurate to what the filmmaker intended. In the digital color-correction process, a great deal of refinement and correction can still be made to each final shot.

When everything looks good to the filmmakers, the movie can be duplicated into several master copies, or "clones," of the original film. These clone versions can be loaded into a film printer to print the images, one frame at a time, onto motion-picture stock for normal film projection. A clone can also be used to create multiple digital versions of the film, which can be projected with a filmless digital projector. At this point, a version of the film will be prepared for DVD, Blu-ray Disc, television, and downloadable release.

Coming Soon to a Theater Near You

The weeks leading up to the release of a film are filled with last-minute adjustments and polishes. In the last year of production, a film is often previewed three or four times to find out what a real audience will think of it. Even if you look back at the earliest days of Walt Disney and Mickey Mouse, you can see that promotion and marketing were always a central part of the business of animation. During the final year of a film's development, the marketing team is hard at work with their plans to promote the film around the world.

What is new and special about this film? How can you capture that "specialness" in one or two images that make the audience want to see this movie over all others? Billboards and TV spots are crucial, but so are the books, products, and toys that the audience will want to take home with them. Publicists work with magazines and television shows to crank up excitement as the premiere approaches. Every image, every product, every interview has to contribute to the event of the movie with the highest quality and integrity.

ABOVE AND RIGHT: The Seven Dwarfs make their appearance at the opening of *Snow White and the Seven Dwarfs* in 1937 at the Carthay Circle theater; OPPOSITE: *Finding Nemo* is marketed on bus shelters, billboards, and local transportation (TOP); crowds packed Central Park in New York for the premiere of *Pocahontas* (NEAR LEFT AND TOP RIGHT); Wynonna Judd performs at the *Lilo & Stitch* premiere (BELOW RIGHT).

Eventually, this leads up to the moment of truth: opening night, when the lights go down and the finished movie is shared with the general public for the first time. An animated film is the ultimate paradox: on one hand, it takes years of work and millions of hours of passion and labor to produce. On the other hand, you want the audience to completely forget all the technology, craft, and hard work that is poured into a film, and simply sit back and enjoy the illusion. The audience response to animation, as with any art form, is an emotional one. Animation speaks to the heart, regardless of language or technique—and when it works, it can inspire and entertain like no other medium.

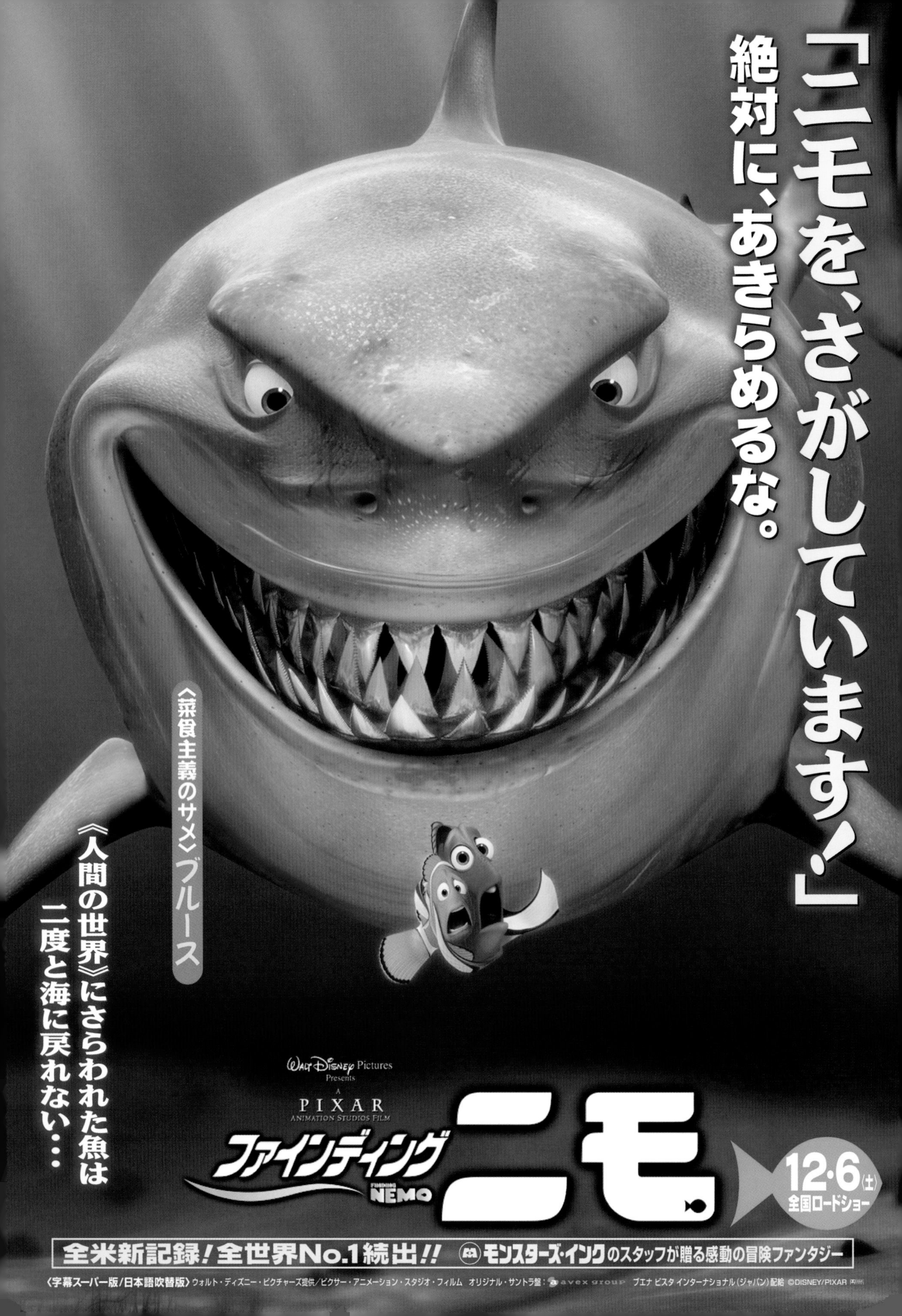

「ニモを、さがしています！」絶対に、あきらめるな。

《菜食主義のサメ》ブルース

《人間の世界》にさらわれた魚は二度と海に戻れない…

Walt Disney Pictures
Presents
A
PIXAR
ANIMATION STUDIOS FILM

ファインディング ニモ
FINDING NEMO

12・6(土) 全国ロードショー

全米新記録！全世界No.1続出!! モンスターズ・インクのスタッフが贈る感動の冒険ファンタジー

〈字幕スーパー版/日本語吹替版〉ウォルト・ディズニー・ピクチャーズ提供／ピクサー・アニメーション・スタジオ・フィルム　オリジナル・サントラ盤：avex group　ブエナ ビスタ インターナショナル(ジャパン)配給 ©DISNEY/PIXAR

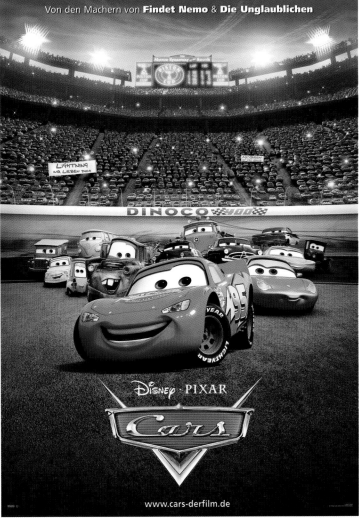

THESE PAGES: The event behind the international release of an animated film takes years to plan. One-sheet posters in multiple languages tout the arrival of a new film. Most Disney animated films then go on to have lives of their own as stage shows (*Beauty and the Beast*, *The Lion King*, *Tarzan*, *The Little Mermaid*, and *The Hunchback of Notre Dame*) or as parades and characters in Disney Theme Parks.

Epilogue

Well, that's the end of your backstage journey for now. But there's more to learn about the animation process. If you are determined to make your own films, work at an animation studio, or even if you are just a fan, there are a lot of ways to increase your knowledge and appreciation of this art form.

"Break time" Apr 20/07

PRACTICE

If you love to draw and wonder if you could ever be part of the studio-animation industry, you're in the same shoes that all animators were when they were just starting out. Sometimes people think drawing is a magical gift that some possess and others don't; the truth is, it all comes down to a little bit of talent and a lot of work—and practice, practice, practice!

Professional athletes might practice four to six hours every day, and then train with weights in the gym three times a week, or work with a personal trainer and coach just to get ready for one game. That's the kind of dedication that it takes to succeed as an animator.

Carry a small sketchbook with you at all times and draw from life. Use the sketchbook to write down story or character ideas based on things that you might see on the streets. Sketch while you eat lunch or watch TV. I even draw while I'm reading the newspaper: it's full of photos of people and animals in action and there's lots of paper, so grab a Sharpie and sketch. Drawing is a lifelong vocation. Joe Grant, the designer, storyman, and author of *Dumbo*, worked at the Walt Disney Studios even when he was in his nineties, and he drew every day. To him, an artist could never learn enough or draw enough. It was a lifelong obsession.

START BIG

Be a generalist. If you eventually work in a large animation studio, you'll be asked to specialize in one department. But early in your career, you shouldn't specialize too much. Try to work with everything: draw, board, model, rig, paint, animate, edit. Even if the experience is simple and short, it will give you a big appreciation for all the jobs it takes to make a feature film. It will also help you discover which tasks you enjoy and where your real talents lie.

OPPOSITE: Some samples from Dave Pimentel's personal sketch books; ABOVE: Ollie Johnston goes over a scene of his rough animation (inset) with Andreas Deja.

MENTORS

Find a mentor. Look for somebody whose work you admire either at school or in the animation industry, and follow his or her example. It's okay to copy work in order to learn, too. Find a scene that you like and try to analyze and copy the motion. Find illustrators or graphic artists that you admire and copy their style or color sense. The great masters of painting and drawing did this to learn their craft, and you can do it, too. (Just don't try to pass the work off as your own ideas. Copy as a training tool only.)

FESTIVALS

There are amazing animation festivals around the world. The largest—in Annecy, France—is full of screenings, lectures, a market, and the opportunity to meet others in the field. Ottawa, Canada; Hiroshima, Japan; London, England; and Rio de Janeiro, Brazil also host animation festivals and conferences that will plug you into the state of the art form. Siggraph holds an annual computer graphics conference; it's also a great organization for information on cutting-edge digital technique. Comic-Con in San Diego is one of the world's largest conferences on comic art; the tables at the conference are full of individual artists who have worked in comics, illustration, and animation all their lives. It's great person-to-person contact for a beginning animator.

The centerpiece of most animation festivals is the animated short subject. Shorts are a wonderful source of experimental animation. Each year, dozens of animated shorts are produced using every imaginable style and technique: 2-D, 3-D, and stop-motion, as well as more unconventional media, like clay, pins, silhouettes, and oil paint. One animator even works with different colored teas. They are usually available at film festivals or for download on the Web, and they can be *really* inspiring. Also, search for Oscar-nominated shorts on the Web to scan the best of the best shorts from past years.

ABOVE AND RIGHT: International animation festival catalogue covers from Annecy, France, and Hiroshima, Japan.

THE ALCHEMY OF ANIMATION

> "The more you are like yourself, the less you are like anyone else, which makes you unique."
>
> —*Walt Disney*

THIS PAGE: Korean animator Hyun-Min Lee studied animation at Cal Arts. These early student drawings inspired her to complete an animated short called *The Chestnut Tree* (BELOW), which led to a job at Disney Animation Studios.

JUMP IN NOW

How do people get a job in animation? Three words: jump in now. If you are interested in working for a large film studio, be willing to jump into anything or any job. You may have to start by delivering coffee and donuts (I did), but it will give you access to the professionals who work in animation. If you have skills, they will recognize it and you'll advance. And sadly, if you're talented but lazy, they will recognize that, too.

It's not easy to "jump in." You have to stay in constant contact with recruiters. You have to be the champion of your own work. You have to work on your resume and portfolio, attend conferences, and be persistent. Most of all, you have to believe that you have something to contribute to the art form.

It's important to recognize that small studios have a lot to offer, too. Commercial houses have to change styles with each job, and they usually have tiny crews of generalists who know how to do a little bit of everything. The video game industry is one of the largest sectors of the animation industry, and gaming studios are dynamic environments for animation artists.

We started this book with the idea that humans have always been searching for a way to bring their drawings to life with a sense of motion and emotion. Animation is the highest form of this ancient, almost genetic desire to bring things to life—to be the creator of amazing worlds populated by amazing beings. It's a great world. Jump in now.

Visual development by Walt Peregoy for *One Hundred and One Dalmatians*.

Glossary of Terms

2-D Animation—Traditional hand drawn animation.

3-D Animation—Computer generated animation.

ADR—Automated Dialogue Replacement. The process of playing back the film as the actor reads a line to the performance on the screen.

Algorithm—A series of steps or instructions that are used to carry out a task.

Animation Paper—Rectangular drawing paper with holes punched in the bottom, which keep individual animation drawings in registration to each other.

Animator—An artist/actor who creates a series of drawings or frames that brings a character to life by establishing the personality, movement, emotion, and attitude of a character.

Armature—An engineered metal skeleton that fits inside a stop-motion puppet.

Art Director—An artist who is responsible for the visual look and design of the entire movie.

Artistic Coordinator—A trouble-shooter/artist who deals with artistic and technical issues on a 2-D film.

Aspect Ratio—The ratio of screen height to screen width. Older films have a 1 to 1.33 aspect ratio (more square in format). Most modern movies have a 1 to 1.85 aspect ratio (more rectangular, like a plasma TV). Wide-screen movies have a 1 to 2.35 aspect ratio.

Associate Producer—The person who deals with production issues including people, time, money, etc.

Attributes—The surface qualities or characteristics that affect the visual representation of a character, set, or object.

Axis—A direction in three-dimensional space. The x-axis usually measures from side to side, the y-axis measures up and down, and the z-axis measures depth.

Background—Painting or set that appears behind the animated characters.

Blue Sketch—Tracing that shows the path of action of an animated character after animation is done. Used by 2-D layout and background artists so they can plan props and lighting that won't interfere with the character's movement.

Breakdown—Intermediate drawing between the animator's key extreme drawings.

Bump Map—Texture map that simulates raised or bumpy surfaces without altering the surface geometry to which it is applied.

CAPS—Computer Animation Production System, Disney Animation's Academy Award–winning system for organizing artwork and scenes, providing artwork to artists, and tracking changes to the artwork through a production. Developed in the 1980's, CAPS is now an obsolete system that has been replaced by off-the-shelf software that does essentially the same thing.

Casting—Process of finding the right person to play a role.

Cel—The clear celluloid on which the characters were painted during the animation process. The painted celluloid, or cel, was placed over a background and photographed, becoming one frame of the animated film.

CGI—Computer Generated Imagery; most often called just CG for computer generated (a CG film, or a CG special effect).

Checking—Most common in 2-D animation, the process of looking at all of the art and camera movements in an individual scene to insure that everything is properly done before it moves on to the next production step. Scenes are checked twice in the process—Animation Check when a scene is still in pencil drawings and Final Check when a scene is completely in color and ready to go to film.

Clean-up—The art of refining an animator's rough expressive drawings into the final detailed drawings that will be scanned and painted to create the final color scene.

Color Key—A painting or small color sketch that illustrates what a particular sequence will look like in the final movie.

Color Model—Part of the process where character colors are assigned. Also a stage where characters, backgrounds, special effects, and computer-graphics elements are all previewed together for the first time for the art director to make adjustments and color choices.

Comparative Size Sheet—Drawing of each character side by side so that the artists can understand character's height and relationship to other characters.

Composer—Musician who writes music for the film

Compositing (sometimes called "Comping")—Digitally combining multiple levels of artwork while applying operations. Elements are assembled in levels according to an exposure sheet.

Contact Shadow—Shadow that the character casts onto the ground or another object. Created digitally, or animated by an effects animator.

Coordinate System—Allows you to locate anything in space by its position on the x, y, and z axis (horizontal, vertical, and depth).

Credits or Screen Credits—Listing of the names of people who worked on the film.

Curve—Path through three-dimensional space defined by a series of points.

Dailies—In modern usage, a screening of that day's work. The directors and crew look at this film (both final color and rough unfinished animation or previz tests) for critique and comment. (Origin: the daily shipment of film from the film lab.)

Deformers—Three-dimensional object, which is used to change the shape of another 3-D object, usually by how closely one is moved to another. Deformers are often used to create face shapes, or smooth, organic-looking movements in an object.

Demo—Early, rough version of a song, usually with just a piano or synthesizer and voice.

Development—Process of exploring an idea for a movie with writers and artists.

Digital Film Print—Process of transferring a scene from digital data to motion picture film.

Director—Creative leader of a project; he or she coaches the actors, artists, and writers.

Displacement Map—Texture map that describes fine surface detail that would be impractical to model geometrically.

Dissolve or Cross-dissolve—Effect of one scene fading out as the next scene fades in.

Dolby—Trade name for a system designed to reduce the noise level of a tape or optical recording. This company is heavily involved in both sound and stereo 3-D presentation.

Draft—Document that describes in detail each individual scene in the movie including the length of the scene (in feet and frames), the name of the animator, and a description of the action in the scene.

Dub (also called Dubbing or Mixing)—Process of combining sounds together until the right balance of dialogue, music, and sound effects is achieved.

Dynamics—Simulated forces, such as rain, wind, or gravity, which act upon particles or surfaces to create realistic-looking motion representing things such as fire, clothing, or surfaces colliding.

Editorial—Department responsible for all of the film and sound elements on a project. The supervising editor is a creative collaborator with the director to make sure the pacing of the film works.

Effects Animator—Adds the forces of nature and physical phenomena to production scenes. Also animates CG props, furniture, and even vehicles such as boats, chariots, carts, and canoes.

Clean-up and effects animation for an *Aladdin* scene.

Effects or Special Effects—Anything that moves but is not a character on the screen is called an effect. Effects animators create the drawings for these special effects in much the same way character animators create characters.

Extreme—Animator's drawing that shows the extreme limits of an action. A scene of animation would be made up of several animator's extreme drawings. Also known as key frames.

Field—What the camera sees. In 2-D production, artwork must be drawn within the field for it to appear on-screen.

Flipping—In 2-D animation, using the non-drawing hand to change quickly between drawings to see how the animation works.

Foley—Process of recording live sound effects while the film is being projected.

Footage—Footage often refers to the amount of footage a person or department has created in a given week. Film is measured in feet and frames or footage. Sixteen frames equal one foot—ninety feet per minute of film.

Frames—Motion picture film is made up of a string of individual pictures or frames that, when viewed in rapid succession, create the illusion of movement. There are twenty-four frames per second of film.

Geometry—The points, lines, angles, and shapes that make up a three dimensional object.

Head—The beginning to a piece of film.

Hi-rez/Low-rez Models—A low-resolution version of a 3-D model is shown with fewer curves or polygons than the model actually has. It can be very useful for reducing the amount of time the computer needs to render a frame during modeling or animation and lets the computer run faster. The high-resolution version of an object includes all the detail of the model and is used for final screen images.

Inbetween—The drawings between the animators' key drawings. Artists who create these drawings are called inbetweeners. In 3-D animation, the computer aids the animator in generating these frames.

Issuing—Meeting between animator and director when a scene or group of scenes are discussed in detail and given to the animator to begin work.

Key—Important drawing or painting that establishes the look of the surrounding artwork.

Key Frame—The position and state of a 3-D element at one point in time. For example, an animator will define a series of key frames that represent extremes of a movement, then the computer can help move the object from key frame to key frame. Also known in 2-D as "extremes."

Layout—Pencil drawings of the stage upon which the animated character will move.

Level—Artwork is sorted into different levels of drawings, i.e., the background level, the character level, the shadow level, the overlay level.

Lighting—Placing computer-simulated lights into a 3-D environment.

Lighting Artist—Creates the look of individual elements and entire scenes, including the creation of textures or subtle use of virtual lights to enhance the mood and tone of a scene.

Live Action—Motion picture photography of real people and things.

Look Development TD—Technical director who works as part of a look-development team to define all the technical aspects needed to create the look of a 3-D element.

Maquette—A very detailed sculpture of a character to help the animators, modelers, and lighters understand the shapes and proportions from every angle. In stop-motion animation, the final sculpt of a character.

Mask/Matte—Isolated part of an image to which you want to apply changes or to protect from changes.

Maya—A widely used 3-D animation and modeling software.

Mix—The adjustment of individual sound elements to create a pleasing, final combination of sounds.

Mocap (short for Motion Capture)—A technique to capture a live performance and turn it into digital data to drive a CG character. Also known as performance capture.

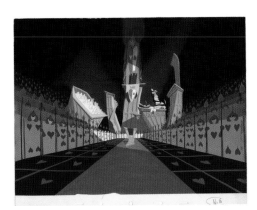

Background painting for *Alice in Wonderland*.

Model Development TD—Technical director who creates all the non-character motion systems for a shot. This may include prop animation, particle systems, or procedural animation.

Model Sheet—Collection of drawings that illustrate how a character is to be drawn.

Modeler—Creates complex, organic models needed for CG character animation, prop elements for effects, and virtual sets for layout.

Motion Blur—Blurring effect of fast motion on the screen; can be digitally replicated by the computer.

Motion TD—Technical director who creates skeletal and other character animation systems, working with character animators and modelers to define the animation system used for their film.

Multiplane—A camera set up with several levels of artwork that could move independently to create the illusion of depth. Computers can now create similar effects.

Muscle/Skin—System used to make a 3-D character's skin surface look like it is moving over actual muscles underneath.

Music Editor—Person who makes sure the music written by the composer fits properly, or in sync, with the picture. This person also keeps track of all musical elements on the show.

Ones—If drawings are done for every frame of film, it's referred to as being on ones.

Orthographic View—View of three-dimensional space that does not show any changes in perspective. Used on architectural and set design plans and elevations.

Outline—Written document explaining in outline form how each act and each sequence will move the story forward.

Overlap—Secondary action, i.e., overlapping hair.

Overlay—Additional drawing or painting on top of the layout or background that illustrates a foreground object.

Pan—Movement of the camera from side to side.

Particles—Points in 3-D space that can be treated as objects, given different sizes, colors, transparency, and so on. For example, millions of particles can create a dust storm or a snowstorm.

PDM (Production Department Manager)—Manages various departments in animation and reports to the Production Manager. Occasionally called APM for Assistant Production Manager.

Pegs—The round and rectangular pegs that hold animation paper in registration.

Photo realistic—Rendering where an object look as realistic as possible.

Pixel—The smallest picture element in a television or digital image composed of red, green, and blue elements. A pixel can only be a single color.

Plates—Live-action backgrounds.

Plussing—Disney term for improving through iteration.

Polygon—Areas defined by three or more points in space.

Pose—Drawing that shows a character in a particular attitude. Also refers to the animators' extreme drawings, i.e., there are five poses in this scene.

Predub—Process of combining sound elements prior to a final dub. Volume levels and sound treatments are often set on sound effects alone before they are combined with dialogue and music. This would be called an effects predub.

Preview—Screening of the film for audience reaction, before the film is completed.

Producer—Person who supervises the making of the film.

Production Auditor—Person who tracks time, productivity, and the expenditure of money for a film.

Production Manager—Person who coordinates the workflow through all departments on a production and also manages the director's schedule.

Production Software TD—Technical director who creates software to help solve the creative requirements of a film.

Quotas—The weekly amount of work that needs to be accomplished in order for the movie to be completed on time.

Release Date—Day that the movie is released to be screened in theaters.

Render—Process of calculating all the parameters of an object or scene to produce an image.

Resolution—How much information is contained in an image. Typically, resolution is measured by how many pixels (counted horizontally and vertically) there are in an image.

Rig—Collection of controls allowing you to animate a model. The controls could be deformers, handles, or any other element allowing you to change the model or its position in space.

Rims—Thin band of light on an edge of a character.

RIO Render input/output—Disney department responsible for the administration and monitoring of the render queue.

Rolling—Method of placing a drawing between each finger and rocking them back and forth to see if the perceived motion is smooth.

Rotate—To change the side of the object facing you.

Rotation—The tilting of the camera field.

Rough—Drawing that is done quickly and expressively to get an idea on paper.

Scale—To change the size of the object.

Scanning—Process of digitizing a drawing into a computer so that it can be painted and combined with other drawings.

Scene—Individual cut in an animated film.

Scene Planning—In 2-D animation, the process of planning out how the background, characters, and effects will be combined, and how the camera and artwork will move to create a sense of reality.

Script—Writer's document that spells out the action, stage direction, and dialogue for a drama. Also known as a screenplay.

Sequence—A chunk of storytelling usually centered on a particular location or piece of business, such as the ballroom sequence, the chase sequence, or the happy-ending sequence.

Server—A computer that makes data and resources available to other computers.

Shader—A short software program or file that specifies how a 3-D object should look, including transparency, color, texture, specularity, reflective properties, and so on.

Shot (sometimes called a Scene)—An individual cut in a live-action movie.

Slate—Identifier at the beginning of a scene that lists the sequence and scene number, animator's name, and other critical information about the scene. (Origin: from the live-action world in the days when this information was written with chalk on a slate and held in front of the camera.) Also an audio slate can be given by the editor to identify who and what is being recorded at a dialogue session.

Sound Effects Editor—Person who finds or creates all of the audio effects for a film and synchronizes them with the picture in preparation for the final sound mix.

Sound Reading—A frame-accurate transcription of a vocal performance. The sound reading will be used by the animator to move the character in sync with a line of dialogue.

Sound Track—An audio timeline (formerly on film, now on a digital track) that contains sounds such as dialogue or sound effects. The timeline runs in sync with the picture.

Spline—Curve that connects the points of a mathematical expression with a high degree of smoothness.

Squash and Stretch—Term to describe the constant tension and release of facial features or physical features on an animated character.

Stats or Photostats—Historically, the frame-by-frame enlargements of live action study film used for reference.

Stereo 3-D—Process where the audience wears glasses to view a three dimensional version of the film on the screen. A digital projector displays two images (right eye, left eye) and the glasses "decode" those images so the film appears to be three-dimensional.

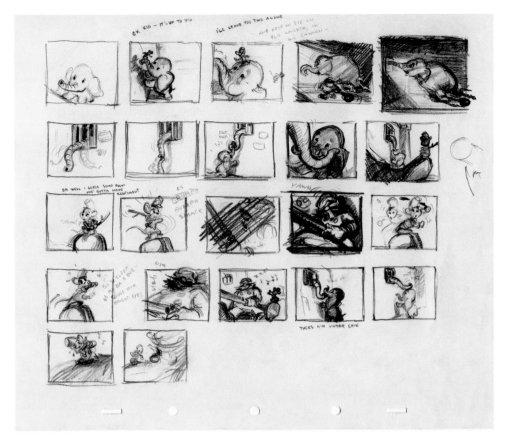

Dumbo thumbnail storyboard.

Storyboard—Sequence of sketches pinned or displayed digitally in consecutive order to tell a story.

Supervising Animator—Animator in charge of a particular character in a movie.

Sweatbox—Meeting with the directors and key artists to critique individual scenes in the film. Named after Walt Disney's Moviola room that didn't have air conditioning.

Sync (short for Synchronous)—Elements of picture and sound being played together at the same time.

Tail—The end to a piece of film.

Texture Map—Digital painting that is applied to a 3-D object in order to give the surface more detail or to describe some attribute of the surface such as transparency.

Texture Painter—A person who creates textures for 3-D models.

Timing Chart—A chart that indicates the timing between key frames of animation.

Tone Mattes—Artwork created by an effects animator that gives a dark or shadowed side to a character.

Track—Individual sound element that runs in sync with the picture. There are multiple tracks for dialogue, music, and sound effects. Also used in music recording with the same meaning i.e., a trumpet track, a cello track, a percussion track.

Tracking—Replicating a real live-action camera move in a digital environment to which 3-D objects (special effects or characters) can be added.

Truck—Movement of the animation camera in and out.

Twos—In certain scenes of animation, an animator can do twelve drawings for every second of film instead of the usual twenty-four drawings. Each drawing is shot for two frames (on twos) and the result still appears to be full animation. Often used in 2-D and stop-motion animation.

Underscore—Music written to play under scenes of action or dialogue.

Virtual set—Three-dimensional movie set allowing a virtual camera to move around in 3-D space.

Visual Effects Editor—Wrangles visual effects shots in a live action film.

Wireframe—A "birdcage" view of a 3-D model, which shows only the curves or lines that make up the object, not the surfaces. It can sometimes be faster to work with the wireframe model, because the computer does not have to constantly calculate what the whole surface should look like. You can also use the wireframe when you want to see both the part of the model facing toward you and the part facing away from you.

Workbook—A technical version of the storyboard with sketches that show how each shot will look in the final film.

X-sheet (short for Exposure Sheet)—Document that keeps track of all of the drawings and camera movements in an animation scene.

Additional Reading

Acting for Animators by Ed Hooks, Heinemann Drama.
Brad Bird writes the forward for this book on acting principles and theory for animators.

Animation from Script to Screen by Shamus Culhane.
A classic animation text by one of the masters of the Golden Age of animation.

Animation from Pencils to Pixels: Classical Techniques for the Digital Animator by Tony White, Focal Press.
This is a big, readable, easy-to-navigate overview of animation production for the digital animator.

The Animator's Survival Kit by Richard Williams, Faber & Faber.
A landmark book on the fundamentals of animation, full of the wit and genius of Richard Williams, director of animation for the Academy Award–winning Who Framed Roger Rabbit.

The Art and Flair of Mary Blair by John Canemaker, Disney Editions.
The story behind one of Walt Disney's favorite artists. Mary Blair was the prolific art director and designer behind films such as Cinderella, Peter Pan, and Melody Time.

The Art of Spirited Away by Hayao Miyazaki, VIZ Media LLC.
Artwork, stills, sketches, storyboards, and illustrations from Miyazaki's Oscar-winning film. No one tops Miyazaki as a modern master of 2-D animation.

Bill Peet: An Autobiography by Bill Peet, Houghton Houghton Mifflin.
A frank insight into the creative process of a story artist, warts and all, and a terrific introduction to the work of one of Disney's best story artists. Bill Peet's storybooks are also a gold standard for any aspiring sketch artists.

Cartoon Animation: The Collector's Series by Preston Blair, Walter Foster Publishing.
Probably the one book responsible for starting more animation careers than any other book. A must-have for animation students.

Creating 3-D Animation: The Aardman Book of Filmmaking by Peter Lord and Brian Sibley, 2004; Harry N. Abrams; revised edition.
Required reading by students of stop-motion animation and animation junkies in general. Featuring the work of Aardman Animation, makers of Wallace and Grommit, Chicken Run, and Creature Comforts.

Creating Characters with Personality: For Film, TV, Animation, Video Games, and Graphic Novels by Tom Bancroft, Watson-Guptill.
Tom is a Disney alumni animator who explores personality-driven character design. Check out the guest contributions by artists Glen Keane, Mark Henn, Jack Davis, and Peter deSève.

Digital Lighting and Rendering by Jeremy Birn, New Riders Press; 2nd edition.
Jeremy is a lighting technical director at Pixar, where he's worked on Cars and The Incredibles. He has taught at Cal Arts and Academy of Art University in San Francisco. A great primer on CG lighting.

Disney Animation, The Illusion of Life by Frank Thomas and Ollie Johnston, Disney Editions.
The animation process clearly explained with amazing illustrations from two masters of Disney's Golden Age of animation. Another must-have for students of animation.

Disney's Nine Old Men and the Art of Animation
by John Canemaker, Disney Editions.
The candid stories behind the lives and art of Walt
Disney's most celebrated animators.

Enchanted Drawings: The History of Animation
by Charles Solomon, Random House; revised edition.
edition. "Any sufficiently advanced technology is
indistinguishable from magic." Arthur Clark's quote
begins this thorough, well-illustrated text on the
history of animation up through the 2-D golden
age of the 1990s.

Human and Animal Locomotion, Volume 1 & 2
by Eadweard Muybridge, Dover Publications;
new edition.
The bible of human and animal locomotion from
one of the pioneers of action analysis and motion
pictures.

Paper Dreams: The Art and Artists of Disney Storyboards
by John Canemaker, Disney Editions.
Storyboarding is a technique developed by the
Walt Disney Studio and used by everyone from
Alfred Hitchcock to Martin Scorsese. Canemaker
focuses on the birth and progression of an
animated film on storyboards.

Prepare to Board by Nancy Beiman, Focal Press.
A comprehensive textbook on storyboarding and
character development. Nancy is a veteran writer,
animator, and story artist who brings her global
experience to this lavishly illustrated book.

Producing Animation by Catherine Winder and Zahra
Dowlatabadi, Focal Press.
One of the only books on the art of producing an
animated film.

*Secrets of Oscar-winning Animation: Behind the Scenes
of 13 Classic Short Animations* by Olivier Cotte,
Focal Press.
A rare insight into the genius, joy, and magic of
independent animated filmmaking.

*Story: Substance, Structure, Style and the Principles of
Screenwriting* by Robert McKee, ReganBooks.
An industry standard, this book is packed with
detailed story analysis for the aspiring screenwriter
and story artist.

*Thinking Animation: Bridging the Gap Between 2-D
and CG* by Angie Jones and Jamie Oliff, Course
Technology PTR.
This book is jammed with history, technique, and
process in a well-illustrated package by two very
talented animators. Angie and Jamie span the
world of animation from 2-D to 3-D and have
experience and insight to spare.

*Tim Burton's Nightmare Before Christmas: The Film, the
Art, the Vision* by Frank Thompson, Disney Editions.
This making-of book documents the process
behind Tim Burton's perennial stop-motion
masterpiece.

Timing for Animation by Harold Whitaker and John
Halas, Focal Press; new edition.
In his Amazon review, John Lasseter says, "The
principles of timing laid out in this book are more
applicable now than ever before."

Vilppu Life Drawing Manual by Glenn Vilppu,
Lightfoot Ltd.
Glenn is the modern master of figure drawing for
animation. This is one of several books and videos
from this great teacher.

Fantasia **storyboard art.**

Acknowledgments

Special thanks to John Lasseter, Ed Catmull, and the entire team at Disney/Pixar Animation Studios. To Wendy Lefkon, Jody Revenson, and Jessica Ward for their undying support of this book and their patience with me. To my Stone Circle team of Connie Thompson, Maggie Gisel, Tracey Miller-Zarneke, and Josh Gladstone.

The breathtaking imagery in this book is courtesy of Lella Smith, Mary Walsh, and the crew of the Disney Animation Research Library: Doug Engalla, Ann Hansen, Jackie Vasquez, Scott Pereira, the amazing Fox Carney, and Tammy Crosson. Grateful acknowledgment to Mike Belzer for his comprehensive behind-the-scenes photographs. And to Hans Bacher and Andreas Deja for loaning us works from their collection.

Thanks also to the tireless Charles Solomon, Tenny Chonin, Kiran Joshi, Patti Conklin, and Steve Goldberg for reading and fact-checking the technical details.

The author and producers would also like to thank Guy Cunningham, Sharon Krinsky, and Sara Liebling, and offer a big thanks to Jonathan Glick for his impeccable design.

Our gratitude to Walt Disney Studios: Andrea Recendez, Angela D'Anna, Christine Cadena, Christine Chrisman, Clark Spencer, Dale Kennedy, Dan Molina, Dave Bossert, Dave Smith, Ed Squair, Elizabeth Wright, Emily Hoppe, Fred Tio, Ginger Chen, Holly Clark, Holly Smith, Kari Miller, Katherine "Kat" Ramos, Kent Gordon, LaToya Morgan, Lawrence Gong, Marissa Messier, Mary Beech, Paul Briggs, Peter Del Vecho, Rikki Chobanian, Robert Tieman, Roy Conli, Scott Seiffert, Steven Clark, Terry Moews, Tia Mell, and Tom Powell. Deep appreciation to Pixar Animation Studios: Kathleen Chanover, Aidan Cleeland, Christine Freeman, Leigh Anna MacFadden, Juliet G. Roth, Peggy Tran-Le, and Mark Walsh.

And finally, to the hundreds of artists who have contributed to the Disney and Pixar canon and have pushed the bounds of an art form for decades.